RAYMOND FOXALL

THE LITTLE FERRET

NEW YORK

ST. MARTIN'S PRESS, INC.

AUTHOR'S NOTE

MANY of the characters in this book were living persons, and to indicate what may be actual history and what may not I list those who are not at all imaginary:

Harry Adkins was one of the cleverest of the Bow Street Runners, and his services were sometimes called upon by the government. His nickname was in fact The Little Ferret. Sir Richard Ford, assisted by Mr. James Read, founded the horse patrol, and Mr. Day did command it, while Mr. Stafford was inspector of the foot patrol.

I need scarcely record as figures of history Admiral Lord Nelson, Lady Hamilton and Mr. Pitt, but in addition to these the then First Lord of the Admiralty, the naval officers mentioned, Lord Nelson's brother and other visitors to Merton were all real people. Thomas Cribb was in fact Nelson's head gardener.

The British Navy prevented the French invasion flotillas from ever sailing, and the end of Nelson in particular, who was feared by the French admirals, was Napoleon's dearest wish.

Lady Hamilton did put a flower in her hair whenever she received a letter from Nelson, and she familiarized members of the household with its text; and it is an historical fact that at their home, just prior to Trafalgar, both spoke freely of the strategy he would employ, and details of this were consequently known to the French Admiral Villeneuve before the battle took place.

BIBLIOGRAPHY

The History of the Bow Street Runners by Gilbert Armitage
Memoirs of a Bow Street Runner by Henry Goddard
Hue and Cry: Birth of the British Police by Patrick Pringle
The Thief-takers by Patrick Pringle
Criminals Confess by Belton Cobb
The First Detectives by Belton Cobb
A Portrait of Lord Nelson by Oliver Warner
Nelson by Carola Oman
Mrs. Jordan, Portrait of an Actress by Brian Fothergill
Leather Face by John Dickson Carr
History of Everyday Things in England by Marjorie &
    W. H. D. Quennell
The Story of Police, Law and Order (Dumpleton)
New Study of Police History (Reith)

PROLOGUE

THE little smuggler turned slowly into the wind, and the man from France, clinging to the dipping gunwale, caught a glimpse of the English coast at its most forbidding. Shortly before dawn on a moonless night was no time to gain a favourable impression of a country to which he sailed on a lonely and desperate venture. For the one moment the cliffs lay dark and distant, a long, grey smudge in the first half-light; but the next instant, mysteriously, there might have been no landfall at all, for as the vessel's sole passenger shaded his eyes against rain and stinging salt-spray, there was only sea again as far as his eyes could see.

"Sacré bleu!" he exclaimed in a whisper, and then checked his tongue abruptly as he realized that on this mission he was to discipline himself to renounce every syllable of his own tongue and speak only English.

Not that he would have any difficulty with the language, for he was no stranger to England, having sheltered there for years as an *émigré* when the rampaging *sans-culottes* were searching for his kind to offer in sacrifice to the insatiable Madame Guillotine. As a boy, the son of a hated aristo, he had been spirited away from Paris to live in London.

It had been a cold, dark dawn on that day, too, and he had gazed at the growing coastline with youthful eyes and no particular emotions. The memory of it had faded. The years had passed, and France recovered some sanity. As a young man he had returned to worship at the feet of the great Napoleon Bonaparte—and serve him. And now it was as though he saw England from afloat for the first time . . .

This time there *were* thoughts, and they were dark and shadowy as the night, and as the cliffs themselves—and touched by something inexplicable that had brought the oath hissing from his lips.

"*Sacré bleu!*" This time he repeated the words to himself.

"To the mains'l, you lubbers!" The words came bellowing from the smuggler's captain, and the crew took their eyes from the tall stranger as they jumped to their duties.

On this night voyage from Calais in the spring of 1805 they had watched the strange gentleman whenever they were allowed to relax. They had noted that though his broadcloth overcoat was a civilian one he bore himself as though he wore a uniform. He had sat in the stern with an unmistakable military bearing, erect and straight-backed yet with ease and grace, as though he were in the saddle—to which indeed he was well used. They had listened carefully when their captain had made an observation to him, and always the stranger's reply had been made incisively and with an economy of words, as though he opened his lips only to eject a command.

When they had put in to France they had been surprised to find that this man was to be their sole cargo.

"He's a Frenchie, and that's all ye need to know," their skipper had said. "And don't let me see ye tryin' to speak to him, or I'll lay about ye with a belaying pin. Aye, and one word out o' your rotten mouths o' this night's work and not one o' ye will sail with me again."

At last the long smudge on the horizon swung into view again and stayed there, growing darker and clearer as the vessel came in.

Suddenly a point of light stabbed out from the land, a solitary gleam on the frowning coastline. Once, twice, thrice it flickered and winked and went out. And the smuggler's captain grabbed a lantern, already lighted and to hand, and swung it from side to side three times in answer before replacing it on the deck beneath the gunwale.

Soon the smuggler was heaving to, and in the slowly breaking dawn they saw before them no port to make, nothing but cliffs and creeks and the lonely, wheeling gulls.

Just audible above the creek of wood and the wind's whip came the splash of oars, and everyone knew that a small boat came rolling out. It came furtively before the night drained out, as it came often for their brandy and their baccy. But this time it put out for their one passenger, who had an air about him that they could not quite understand.

The sailors strained their ears. Now they would learn the name of their passenger. *The Vicomte de Boulogne? Monsieur le Bret?* Those were the sort of names they expected to hear.

But when the boat was made fast to the vessel a voice hailed them. "Mr. John Bellamy?" it asked.

"The same," replied the man whose real name was *Capitaine le Vicomte de St. Remy.*

He climbed down into the boat, and as it cast off and pulled away, disappearing into a clinging mist patch, the crew of the smuggler knew, suddenly and intuitively, that his real name they would never be likely to learn.

CHAPTER ONE

DARK figures dragged the boat clear of the tide as its keel scraped the shingle, and the man from France stepped on to firm sand and looked quickly about him. In the lonely little bay, carefully chosen by his friends for his arrival on English soil, there was little for him to see in the early dawn save the shadowy outlines of those who awaited him further up the beach.

If they were friends, all would be well. If not, his mission would end before it had begun. And in the misty light before daybreak he could see only their broad-brimmed, tall-fronted Napoleonic hats (that were as English as they were French) and their long, high-collared overcoats. For an instant he hesitated, turning back over the dim-lit water to see the ship that had smuggled him in already moving out to make port—and keep its secret. Then he strode forward towards those who waited.

They were three in number, saluting him with raised right arms, silent and grim-faced as they remembered their own arrival this long time past, since France declared war on England and Holland. That had been in 1793, a month after their King, Louis XVI, had gone to the guillotine. Ever since there had been a state of war, and the Frenchmen who waited in the secluded English bay had lived for years in England, seeming more English than the English, forming bit by bit a network of espionage and smuggling their choicest morsels of intelligence back home across the water.

Now the ambitious Bonaparte was emperor, Napoleon I, the idol of France; and his admirals and generals had with extreme care chosen and despatched to England this mysterious gentleman whom they who waited there had been ordered to address as John Bellamy—and to regard as someone extraordinary in their line of business.

"Mr. Bellamy?" inquired one of the French spies.

"I am John Bellamy," replied the newcomer, without returning their salute, which had seemed a little too military in the circumstances.

The man who had greeted him studied his features closely in the half-light, hoping to see in the arrival an old colleague, or at least a man easily recognizable as some prominent person. He saw beneath the plain black hat the face of a man whose years perhaps approached the thirties, though age was difficult to judge in any who had passed through that time in France known as "The Terror"—and lived.

The dark-moustached face was lean, almost hollow-cheeked, but it was the leanness of fitness and health; the dark eyes burned with intelligent fires, and the nose was long and well-shaped as in the portraits of many ambitious figures of history. It was the face of a man to be reckoned with, thought he who received him on the shore, but quite definitely not one he recognized. It could be dangerous sending a man they did not know . . . why, he could be almost anybody. Still, they had their orders.

"Come," he said to the traveller. "We have horses waiting."

They walked up the beach, with the light growing more rapidly, and climbed a path between boulders until they reached the cliff's top. Here among the windblown gorse stood a fourth man in charge of five horses.

Soon they were mounted and away, thudding over damp earth and clattering at last on to the hard road, with the beat of the tide far off in their wake and the sea-wind dying.

They rode in an unyielding silence, asking no questions nor discussing their business until they halted for breakfast at a lonely inn on the London Road.

Here they asked for a private room, tankards of ale and

14

cold meats. And here the reception committee allowed rein to its curiosity.

"We do not—er, know each other yet," began he who had spoken on the beach. "Let us introduce ourselves. My name is Charles Justice. These fellows are Speed, Swift and Jamieson."

The newcomer bowed, smiling wryly. "The names are a trifle—er, *dramatique*." His superiority over the others was at once obvious.

"They are our names." The speaker was still cautious.

"Come, my friends, not your real ones." The man who called himself Bellamy had taken the most comfortable chair, as of his right, and now his eyes were beginning to twinkle. "You are not required to play games with *me*."

"If they are not our names," Justice allowed, "then we have forgotten those with which we were baptized. And what of your name, sir?"

"Ah, what of it?"

"Is it yours—by birth, sir?"

"It will do well enough. I do not need to tell *you* that it is an assumed name. I will not impart to you my real name—nor my rank—purely so that if you do not know it you may not whisper it where ears may be cocked to listen."

There was an uncomfortable silence, then another question: "Are we allowed to know the nature of your mission?"

"I think not," said Bellamy, crisply. "The task I have been sent to accomplish is of the most drastic. The great emperor believes that if I succeed in one desperate act it will spell the fall of England—and this as you all know he desires almost fanatically. The precise nature of my mission, therefore, I will keep a close secret, at least till the time be ripe."

"Even from us?"

"Even from you. The less who know the better?"

"With us any secret of France is safe."

"In your most sober moments, yes."

15

"In all our moments. Drunk or sober, we do not speak."

The man known as Speed spoke for the first time. "If we are not acquainted with the matter in hand, sir—why, how then can we help you?"

"I shall see I get all the help I require—and yet keep my lips sealed," snapped Bellamy. "I am afraid you will have to trust me, all of you, for it is too big a thing by far to endanger its success by the merest whisper."

A creaking beyond the door brought sudden silence within the room. For a moment the five men stood still, eyeing each other. Then Bellamy strode forward and flung open the door suddenly to reveal nothing more sinister than the innocent, white-capped face of a serving maid whose lips curved in a pretty smile above the tray she carried.

"Enter," commanded Bellamy.

As she made her way to the table, he who was named Swift, a handsome young man who appeared to smile a great deal more than was necessary, assisted her to place the tray on the table. Then he proceeded to slap her bottom and kiss her cheek.

"Mr. Swift!" Bellamy rapped out his name like a pistol shot. "Have you nothing better to do than chase wenches?" When the girl had gone he added sneeringly: "Do you see now why I seal my lips? You'd bed the wench and reveal the secret before you'd even made love to her."

Justice did not at once move to the table. "Do not tell us, then, the precise nature of your task," he said. "But it will be to do with the war, of course?"

"It is certainly to do with the war—very much to do with it."

"It will be to root out some special intelligence?"

"That and more. Much more. But do not, pray, disturb yourselves. I have not been sent to spy on *you*. There is nothing known against you—or your work." A smile flickered, and it was the sort that accompanies a sneer.

Justice was long-faced as he spoke. "You will be wanting some assistance from us?" he inquired.

16

"Yes, beginning at once—with some information."
Bellamy rose and moved to the window, looking out over
the deserted countryside. In the cold morning light there
were to be seen neither house nor man, only an occasional
tree, gaunt and bare and wind-bent.

He appeared to derive some satisfaction from the sight—
and from the fact that already, as he well knew, he had
established a firm superiority over the four men huddled
round the table in the shadowed room.

"What sort of information?" ventured Justice.

"First—of whom are we to beware?"

"For a start, all who move and speak——"

"Naturally, but are there any in particular? Is there any
organized force for law and order—or for the security of the
country?"

"There is the night watch, known as Charlies because
they were first set up in King Charles's day, but they are all
old men and infirm, who take their pension and turn a blind
eye on whatever should pass during the night. There are
hundreds of them, but they are quite useless."

"Is that all?"

"No, there are in the city some five dozen of the **Bow
Street Patrol**. They wear no uniform, but you might recognize them from the arms they carry—carbine, pistol and
cutlass. They are out at night, too, walking London Town,
and they are certainly more to be reckoned with."

"Bow Street? Why Bow Street?"

"Because they are under the direction of the chief magistrate, and he has his office at Bow Street, near Covent
Garden."

"So. And any others?"

"Only the thief-takers. Sometimes known as Fielding's
People, after the magistrate who first set them up, or as
Bow Street Runners after the police office which is their
headquarters. But they are neither armed nor uniformed,
and they but poke their long noses into criminals' affairs."

The contemptuous smile gleamed again and was gone.

"So, that is the complete force mustered against London's criminals? Well, I am glad of it, for I shall make much use of the criminals. I shall consort with the sneak-thieves and pickpockets, the footpads and highwaymen, the men and women who would seem to have no honour in their country —and for a fistful of coins would betray it."

Justice, for the time being, was more at ease. "We have already made use of such folk. They live in their hundreds in a district of London known as Whitefriars. It is to this hell-hole of narrow, filthy streets that the sneak-thieves scurry like rats. It is there, where they are tolerably secure from arrest, that they who ride the highway carry their spoils when they have had their way of the coaches."

"You have friends there still, in this Whitefriars?"

"We do—and they are at your disposal. We shall be pleased to show them to you, and in that part of London you can talk to them in perfect safety. The forces of law and order, such as they are, avoid the place as it were the plague."

"It is the safest place for me to meet your—er, friends?"

Justice smiled. "Yes, it is better for you to go to them rather than bring them to see you. It's a dark place full of evil smells. But if your talk is overheard chances are it would be a person disloyal to King George."

"Who are your contacts in this thieves' den? What type of criminal?"

"All types from pickpocket to murderer."

"Ah! Murderer, eh? And what of the highway robbers? Among your friends are there any who might be said to be —er, well connected?"

"Some."

"Then I think I may put the highwaymen to good use. Those fellows are the boldest of thieves, and they may have also the wit to do my bidding."

There was silence for a time while the ale and meat were devoured. Then, relaxing and lighting a pipe, Bellamy said: "Gentlemen, I will give you my confidence in some

18

part. I will state two reasons for my presence here, though not at this stage the details."

They leaned back in their chairs to listen.

"For one thing, I have news that will greatly excite you," he went on. "Bonaparte means to make this the year he invades England——"

"Mon dieu!" Bellamy's fellow conspirators were on their feet, crowding round his chair, their eyes gleaming, their mouths gaping.

He silenced them with a raised finger, but his eyes caught the fire from theirs. "Not so loud, jumping about so. You will have the landlord sneaking at the keyhole. But it is quite true, gentlemen. Admiral Villeneuve has been told to prepare our ships of the line. He's a key-figure, for this damned island has the sea at its doorstep. Bonaparte has a flotilla and a vast army ready to sail, and England will crack like a rotten shell."

"When will they invade?"

"The date I do not know. Possibly it has not yet been named."

Justice spoke in a low voice. "What is the other thing you can say?" he asked.

"I am here to do what is to be done before the offensive is launched," said Bellamy. "Your work is to root out intelligence. Mine, too. But I am charged with other work in addition. I have to rid this world of they whom Bonaparte hates—they who may most hinder his plans."

"Murder?" breathed Justice.

"Murder, assassination, call it what you will. Quite simply, sir, I am here to kill—for France."

CHAPTER TWO

THE French spy rode for London well content with his talks at the wayside inn, but his smile would have been less broad had he known of a new interest being taken there in the highwaymen he hoped to use.

That very forenoon Sir Richard Ford, the chief magistrate at Bow Street, bent his head the better to hear the whispered information brought in by one of his peace officers. Then he swept off his wig, planted his black hat squarely on his head and adjourned his court. "Lead me to the spot," he ordered. "I shall see it for myself."

It was nothing new for a magistrate to conduct criminal investigations in person, for on his shoulders fell the responsibility for preserving order as well as administering justice. He had to catch the thieves as well as try them. So the premises over which he lorded it contained not only his court of justice; they were known, in fact, as the Bow Street Police Office.

In the last hundred years the population of the metropolis had doubled to a million souls. In the labyrinth of dark alleys crime festered more than anywhere else in England, and for half a century each new magistrate had struggled against the growing evil with his handful of patrolmen and thief-takers and his pitifully small funds.

It was not surprising, therefore, that Sir Richard wore a dark scowl as he accompanied Mr. Harry Adkins, one of the most experienced of his thief-takers, through narrow, cobbled streets to a sedate square of three-storeyed Georgian houses.

Here Adkins the Runner, better known as The Little Ferret, halted at a door and stubbed his forefinger at a paper nailed to it.

"There it is, sir," he said. "Pray read it for yourself."

Sir Richard studied the paper, on which was written in a sprawling hand this message:

LET ALL GENTLEMEN BEWARE!

We hereby give due Notice to such Gentlemen who reside in this House and District and all others of ample means in the Citie and Libertie of Westminster that we are verie angry with a new Fashion with regarde to travelling on the highway.

This is that many are taking about their persons not enough of their Worldlie Wealth. This does but mean that they are unable rightly to pay their rents to us.

And we doe hereby order that no Gentleman shall goe out of the citie by horseback or coach without at least £10 and a gold watch on his person, which goods shall pass to our hands by our request as Gentlemen of the Road. Otherwise such as doe nott obey our Commande shall suffer the most dire penalties at our hands.

This by Order of The Societie of Highway Gentlemen.

The magistrate resisted the temptation to tear the paper away. "Remove it carefully and preserve it, Mr. Adkins," he said instead. "It may be useful as evidence."

Runner Adkins folded the paper and placed it in a pocket of his tail-coat. "Do you not think, sir, that the gentleman of the house should be interviewed?" he said.

"That we shall do at once," came the terse reply. "Knock upon the door, Mr. Adkins."

They were shown to chairs in a sitting-room, where a portly gentleman at once waited on them.

"I am Sir Richard Ford, of Bow Street," said the magistrate. "This is Mr. Adkins, one of my officers. A paper was nailed to your door. Pray show it to the gentleman, Mr. Adkins."

The householder remained standing while he read the message, but paled visibly and took a seat when he had done so.

21

"Do you know why it was placed on your door?" queried Sir Richard.

"I do not, sir."

"Is there any explanation why it should be *your* house that was chosen?"

"I do not like it, sir. I—I do not like it."

"Of course you do not, sir. But 'tis not an answer to my question. Have you at any time recently been molested by a highway robber?"

The gentleman put a hand to his brow. "Indeed I was. My coach was stopped at Blackheath these five days ago by a fellow wearing a mask and well mounted. He robbed me of all he could find. But—but I am afraid he could only discover three guineas in my waistcoat pocket."

"What did he say?"

"He was much annoyed and ordered me to make sure I had more than that about me when next I travelled."

"Did he know your identity?"

"He asked my name—and where my residence was situated."

"And you told him?"

"I did."

Sir Richard rose. "If I may say so, sir, I think you were a trifle unwise. You may yet get a visit from a house-breaker. I will take my leave, but if you receive other such messages, or there be any developments at all, I should be acquainted immediately of such."

"I will most certainly do so, Sir Richard. But I am afraid I shall take warning. I shall have ten pounds at least about me whenever I leave the house."

"As you please," said the magistrate, coldly, "but that is not what we would wish the matter to bring about."

Magistrate and detective returned hurriedly to Bow Street, where Sir Richard postponed all court hearings for the day and ordered an immediate conference.

This was attended by his two assistant magistrates, his

eight officers, or Runners as they were known, and Mr. Stafford, the chief inspector of his foot patrol.

Sir Richard addressed them in the most serious tones. "For six years I have been the chief magistrate here," he said, "and I have seen much done to catch thieves who work on foot. I cannot, gentlemen, say the same of those who go about their business mounted and well armed.

"We have even helped in the matter of armed smugglers, for the Revenue men have applied to us in the past for experienced thief-takers to make investigations and effect arrests.

"But these armed men of the highway would appear to enjoy a complete immunity from our organization. They terrorize the roads leading into London, and there are more there than in the rest of the kingdom put together.

"Why, they are grown so bold as to hold up coaches openly in broad daylight—and that, gentlemen, in St. James's. Their impudence grows day by day. Consider this piece of paper. It was nailed to a gentleman's door. I should like you all to read it carefully.

"In short, gentlemen, the position has become quite intolerable, and I should appreciate your views on the matter."

The paper was passed round, and Mr. James Read, one of the two assistant magistrates, cleared his throat and began to speak. "We have a previous example to study—that of a former justice at this office, Sir John Fielding, he who was known as The Blind Beak.

"Not thirty years ago he wrote a pamphlet which he titled, *A Plan for Preventing Robberies Within Twenty Miles of London,* and another called, *An Account of the Rise and Establishment of the Real Thieftakers.* Mr. Pitt, I remember, was greatly interested in both these works."

"Aye, but did The Blind Beak *do* anything about it?" Harry Adkins put his question plainly.

"He did, Mr. Adkins," replied Read. "He formed a plan he called 'quick notice and sudden pursuit'. He asked twenty gentlemen whose country houses lay within twenty miles of London to send a servant by horse with written particulars the moment they got wind of a highway robbery. He then had a description of the thief printed in the *Public Advertiser,* and I knew of one highway robber who was taken in London but a few hours after holding a coach in Essex."

Sir Richard broke into the conversation. "You make the very point, Mr. Read, that I wished to discuss. Sir John even cajoled the government into allowing monies for the payment of mounted men to patrol the roads into the city. It did much good, but it was a somewhat raggle-taggle force of men who were allowed to take up other work as well as that, and very soon this patrol was disbanded altogether."

The speaker paused, then raised his voice: "What I would like us to study now is this—should we set up once again a horse patrol, but such a one that would be so disciplined and so bold that it would put the fear of the devil into these scum of the highway—and ride them off the roads to damnation."

"A good enough scheme, sir," put in one of the Runners. "But could we have a large enough force at our disposal."

"That may be considered later," replied Sir Richard. "In the first place, do we think it would work? Mr. Stafford, you are in charge of our foot patrol in the city. What are your views, sir?"

Stafford leaned forward. "My own patrol does very well," he said. "Why should not one composed of mounted men?"

"Why not indeed."

"Would you suggest, Sir Richard, that it be run on the same lines as my own patrol?"

"Much the same, Mr. Stafford—but with a difference. I would propose to put such a horse patrol into uniform."

"With respect, Sir Richard, I should be against uniform. My patrol has none, and as you know I have always been against it. I know that my men would be hampered in their duties if they were to wear any distinctive clothing,

24

as would the Runners. For one thing, we are not liked by the public, who think their liberties curtailed by us."

"You are most bold, Sir Richard," said Read. "No man attached to a police office has ever before worn uniform."

"True, but have you not forgotten something?" returned the chief magistrate. "There is a great deal of road to be patrolled on the outskirts of the city, for the highways lead out into four counties, and one might think our men should be at all places at all times. But that is quite impossible.

"How best, then, can we discourage these robbers? By arranging that the roads are not only patrolled but are *seen* to be patrolled."

It was promptly agreed that Sir Richard's scheme was sound, and that he should petition the government for additional funds to pay for such a patrol.

How many men would be enlisted? That would depend on the monies the authorities allowed him.

What type of men would ride for him? The frown that Ford had worn all day was melting into a thin smile, and his eyes were flashing as they did when he examined a witness in his dark-panelled court. "I shall have the best horsemen in the country," he said. "They shall all be troopers who have ridden many a long mile in foreign lands with their wits about them. They shall be tough and sworn to their duty, and they shall ride their quarry into hell."

"Who shall lead them?"

The question was spoken quietly, the answer given in ringing tones. "As to that, gentlemen, it is our first task to find a man of intelligence and courage, like our Mr. Stafford here, one who would give to his task more than he was asked to give. He may be a difficult man to find—but find him we will."

The meeting broke up in a mood of excitement. It was as though they felt themselves on the eve of great events.

As indeed they were. In more ways than one it was a remarkable era . . .

In matters of peace a man called Trevithick, the son of

a Cornish mine manager, had but recently built a locomotive, though it was to be eighteen years before railways
would carry their first passengers. The first steamboats had
appeared, but so far only on a Scottish canal. That very year
a man named Scott had begun to write romantic poems,
though not yet had he begun the famous Waverley novels.

As to war, George III's generals had one in fourteen of
the population under arms for the war with France. And
before the year was to end there was to take place on the
high seas one of the most glorious naval victories the world
had ever known . . .

CHAPTER THREE

THE highwayman's hand tightened on the reins as he watched the solitary horseman jogging sedately towards him. The approaching figure was a gentleman of sorts, for the tall top-hat, long-tailed jacket and booted pantaloons were plainly visible in the noonday distance.

From the clump of trees in whose shade he lurked, it was these things the watcher noted, rather than the rider's easy seat and squared shoulders.

The man in the trees' shade put on his mask, drew a pistol from the saddle-holster—and waited. If a stupid fellow braved the highway alone and unarmed, he must reckon with they who plied their trade on its most sequestered stretches . . .

He who drew near was a Mr. Josiah Day, a peaceable looking individual with his hair neat and his huge, black bow meticulously tied across the peeping white collar jutting at his chin.

He would present, decided the highmayman, not a morsel of trouble with a pistol levelled at his chest.

But the traveller came on with exasperating slowness. He rode as a man might with no business to transact and no acquaintance with danger on an English lane. The man who waited cursed impatiently under his breath, and the hand that held the pistol was not quite steady.

At last Mr. Day came up, his tall, black hat bobbing above the lowest tree branch, one hand light on the reins, the other languidly twirling a long, silver-knobbed cane instead of a crop. In the morning sun his face was placid, expressionless.

"Hold—if you value your life!" The highwayman crashed suddenly from the spinney, and the words rasped from his lips.

He saw that the horse before him was more startled than its rider. And he noted, too, that the animal was controlled instantly. What he did not at once discern was that the eyes before him had narrowed and were glinting warily.

"Do not move—or you are a dead man."

Mr. Day, as it so happened, was not unfamiliar with firearms or the damage they could inflict, having suffered a wound in the leg which had left him somewhat lame.

"You have the advantage of me," he said, and his voice was loud and even. "I am not armed."

"Excellent. Do just as I say, sirrah, and you will come to no harm."

"I am at your command, sir." The traveller doffed his hat and his smile was disconcerting.

"Hey, you, I do not trade in fine manners," snapped the highwayman. It was as though they fenced with imaginary rapiers and a stronger personality was gaining ground on him. This was no paunchy, trembling gentleman, and the bold thief was not so sure of himself as before. "Now quick about it—fling your money and valuables to the ground, and then make off before I put a ball through you."

Mr. Day put a hand to his pocket and two coins tinkled to the ground.

"Huh! That ain't enough. Dig deeper, sirrah."

"Not so fast, my fine fellow. Not so fast." The victim was trying to smile, but a cold, bitter rage was growing within him—and for a very particular reason. "Pray have a little patience. I have a fine gold watch about me, but my heart is greatly attached to it, and if you must have it I would not see it broken by casting it on the ground. Pray allow me to come nearer so that you may make certain of catching it before it falls to the road."

"Hold where you stand!"

"As you please."

"I do not like your manner."

"Nor I yours. But if you would have the watch——"

"Hold! _I_ shall come nearer to _you_."

28

It was not a gold watch, nor yet a silver one, but it gleamed in Mr. Day's hand as the rascal halted his horse a pace or two away.

"Catch! Quickly!" The even tones had gone and the words exploded like orders.

The highwayman's eyes moved for the briefest moment in order to catch the watch, but in that instant Mr. Day catapulted himself into action. His long cane flashed and whistled as it were a cavalry sabre, and the arm that wielded it was strong and sure. Down it thwacked on the barrel of the pistol, which went rattling to the ground without even exploding. Back came the cane for another blow.

But the highwayman's spirit had melted like sleet in spring, and he was wheeling his horse and spurring madly, thudding into a gallop, high in the stirrups and unnerved by the ringing pain in his right hand.

Unnerved, too, by the echoing hooves coming after him in hot pursuit. For the peaceable-looking Mr. Day, wasting not a moment of his advantage, had given heels to his horse and was pounding on behind as though he rode a face.

From his first glimpse of the highwayman a cold, calculated anger had mounted in him. Now he pressed his animal to the limit of its speed.

His was no longer the face of a civilian gentleman going quietly about his business. It was that of a man inflamed with rage and determined that his quarry should not escape him. The eyes burned and the jaw was set. Josiah Day had good reason for hating highwaymen.

The fleeing man whipped a glance over his shoulder and saw his pursuer gaining ground. He drove his spurs viciously into his animal's flanks.

But the man who gave chase was drawing level, and the long cane was aloft, poised like a sabre, its polished wood gleaming like steel in the sunshine. The swish of its descent was lost among the echoes of pounding hooves. But not the crack of the blow on the criminal's arms. The reins flew free of the nerveless fingers.

At the same moment Josiah Day was closing in, jostling the other horse and swerving it to the roadside. Already the masked man, desperately gripping with his knees, was losing balance, and a lunge to the chest with the cane unseated him. With a great yell he toppled.

The other man kept his seat with comparative ease, for it would have taken much to unhorse him. He pulled in his mount, wheeled and rode back to the spot where the fallen man was beginning to struggle to his feet from the soft earth at the side of the road.

Momentarily stunned, the highwayman watched his adversary dismounting quickly, and saw that he limped slightly as he hurried towards him. The criminal made for the gateway to a field, bent on eluding the devil that he had unleashed in this otherwise peaceful-looking individual. Day was covering the ground in an odd, jumping run, but surprisingly quickly for a man whose leg had been weakened by a past wound.

He grabbed the robber, swung him round by the shoulder and crashed his fist into the man's face. The hunted man began to feel like a trapped animal. He put up some fight, but the other dominated him with his cold fury, and he took a painful thrashing.

When it was all over Josiah Day stood over the sprawling, stirring figure, his fists still clenched. "That is for you and all your kind," he panted, and his voice was hard and strained. "You are scum of the devil—the lot of you—and to me you are even worse. It was one of you scoundrels who did me a great wrong. He gave me something to remember for life. I will not trouble your wretched ears with the details——"

He broke off, as though more words were difficult to find or too painful to utter. "I do not know if you are the man who wronged me. Possibly I do not care. All I know is that you are one of a vile breed, and I feel the better for having given you a beating. You of all your fellows will not escape justice. On your feet, sirrah, for I now propose to hand you over to the law. You at least have molested your last traveller."

The man lay on the ground, his mask and hat gone, unable to register any expression through his battered features. But he was not unconscious.

Day picked up the cane he had dropped when he leapt to the ground, and re-mounted his horse.

"On your feet," he roared again. "On your horse—quickly."

When the man was in the saddle again, sitting dejectedly and painfully, his captor said: "I have a mind to regain my watch. We shall return to where it lies on the road."

When they reached the spot he ordered the robber to dismount, and alighting himself, prodded the man forward with his cane until he could recover the watch. He also took possession of the pistol, assuring his captive that it was still in good working order.

Then they rode towards London, Day keeping a wary eye on the disconsolate man by his side, though scarcely needing to do so, for the highwayman's spirit had quite gone.

Josiah Day prodded the highwayman into the Bow Street Police Office with his own pistol, much to the delight of thief-taker Harry Adkins, who listened intently to the tale of the capture and at once conceived an intriguing idea.

"Will you be kind enough to remain seated for a moment?" he said. "I should very much like you to talk with the chief magistrate."

Day took a chair while Adkins went to find Sir Richard Ford. "Reference our proposed horse patrol, sir, there's a character here I should like you to see," he began.

The thief-taker's enthusiasm infected the magistrate. "Done for the scoundrel in excellent style, sir. Dragged him off his horse and gave him what for. Nearly closed both his eyes, and gave him a bloody nose. Then brought him in. There ain't many would do such a thing."

31

"Indeed there are not," agreed Sir Richard, his eyes gleaming.

"Oh, and one thing more, sir—don't be misled, if I may say so, by his agreeable manner. I'd say he has but recently shaved off a fierce moustache. Tells me he was a captain of cavalry."

"Interesting, Mr. Adkins. Very interesting." The magistrate nodded sagely. "Show him in at once, if you please."

Seated before Sir Richard, the visitor did not seem quite so peaceful a character as the thief-taker had suggested. His top-hat was dented and dusty, his huge black bow awry and his silk waistcoat torn. Furthermore, his face bore unmistakable signs of a bout of fisticuffs.

"We are greatly in your debt, sir," said Sir Richard, proffering his snuff-box.

"Glad to be of assistance, Sir Richard." The smile was bland, and the magistrate tried to imagine it topped by a twirling moustache. "But the scuffle with that scoundrel was also something I owed to myself."

"You do not care for highway robbers?"

"I detest them. I have the greatest reason, but it is a personal one. I would rather not speak of it."

"So we shall not, then." For the moment the magistrate changed the subject. "They tell me you held a commission in the cavalry?"

"I did, Sir Richard."

"And you are now a private citizen?"

"I received a pistol ball in the leg in the wars with Bonaparte. I ride well enough, but I am not the same man on my legs. I was not considered fit enough to remain in my regiment. It is unfortunate, for I now seek employment and it is not easy to find."

"If I may say so, Mr. Day, it may not be difficult in your particular case."

"Because I gave a thief a trouncing? Tut, sir, 'twas but a morning's diversion."

Sir Richard's eyes gleamed brighter. "You have done a

good morning's work. It might have been nothing more—
but for one thing. Have I your confidence, Mr. Day, do I
tell you of it?"

"I served my commission truly, sir. I am, I hope, a man of
honour."

"Then I will tell you. The thieves and scoundrels on our
roads into London are now as thick as flies about a midden,
and their audacity has become quite intolerable."

"They are utterly detestable, and I would feign wage a
private war on them!"

"An excellent thought, Mr. Day. But you may yet be
able to make it a public war."

"How so, sir?"

"We are to get up a patrol of horse so that henceforth the
scoundrels may not have it all their own way."

"Excellent, Sir Richard." Josiah Day was on his feet, his
face animated. "If there is any way in which I can help——"

"I am quite sure there is. It has been decided that all
the men we enlist must have served in a cavalry regiment,
that they shall be men of impeccable honour and that they
shall be of the married state."

Day resumed his seat, his smile fading. "As to the last, sir,
I am afraid I cannot comply. I *was* married. But my wife—
no longer—lives."

"I think that in *your* case we could count you in. You
would still be a married man, but for some misfortune."
Sir Richard paused and treated his visitor to a long, keen
gaze.

"But if you are to join our fight against crime, Mr. Day, I
think I should like to know more of the reason why you so
detest these highway robbers. Perhaps you would tell me
more?"

Josiah Day returned the gaze, and there was a long pause,
as though he willed himself to speak. "I was overseas with
my regiment. It would not have happened else, for I would
have been escorting her . . . They sent word to me . . . When
I returned they told me the true facts . . ."

His words waned and he was silent. "She was travelling with friends," he continued at last. "I speak of my wife, Sir Richard. The coach was stopped by one of those curs. A gentleman inside put up some small argument. The thief exploded his pistol. My—wife—was killed."

Sir Richard rose and moved towards his visitor. Without a word he placed a hand on the man's shoulder.

"It may have been an accident." Day's voice had been low and tremulous. Now it flared in well-remembered anger. "I care not if this were so—or not. The man was a murderer just the same. He was masked, and none knows who he was. When he saw what he had done he turned his horse and fled. I do not expect ever to know his name—or meet him face to face. He does not deserve to live, devil's spawn that he is.

"He and his damned fellows, they should be all rooted out, and I'd see every mother's son of 'em to the gallows, did I but have my way."

"I am very sorry, Mr. Day." The magistrate resumed his seat. "Before you told me this story, I had a mind to offer you responsible rank in our patrol. Now that I have heard it, I would like to offer you the very highest. Subject to my checking your army record, Mr. Day, will you take command of such a patrol, enlist the men for it—and lead it with distinction against this intolerable danger on the King's highway?"

The two men rose. Already Sir Richard was extending his hand to grip that of the ex-captain.

"I will do my best," said Day, "and with God's help I will not fail you."

"I had to find just the right man," returned the magistrate. "I am now certain that in you, Mr. Day, I have found him."

CHAPTER FOUR

JOHN BELLAMY, the man from France, arch-spy, assassinator and assumed Englishman, went to Whitefriars on foot. He was led through the narrow streets by his colleague, Justice, who had advised that they both wear clothes drab enough not to provoke undue interest.

After a time Justice indicated a narrow alley. They entered and found it so dark that it was necessary to take each other by the arm so as not to lose contact with each other. Justice, familiar with the place, halted in the blackness and rapped three times on a door. This was opened from within and the pair stepped into a dimly lit corridor. Pacing this, they entered another door, this time into the smoke-filled interior of a very small tavern.

They ordered ale, and as they sipped it the landlord, a hunched and squinting individual, sidled up to them.

"A welcome to my owld 'ouse," he said. "A welcome to be sure." Then he grinned furtively, put his face close to Justice's ear and spoke behind a secretive hand. "Mebbe as 'ow I can be of some 'elp, sir?" he inquired. "Wantin' ter see some of yer owld friends, eh? If there be any one in partickler——"

"Yes, Mr. Fag, he they call Gentleman Jerry."

"Ah, Gentleman Jerry. To be sure, Gentleman Jerry."

"Will he be visiting this night?"

Tom Fag screwed up his mouth in thought. "Now let I see, sir, 'e may be—and then 'e may not."

Justice spun a silver coin with one hand and caught it with the other.

Fag's eyes followed the course of the coin. Then he said: " 'E could allus be sent fur, good sirs, an' 'e would wait on ye punctual, always supposin', that is, 'e weren't out a-riding the roads."

"Well, you do just that, Mr. Fag," ordered Justice, proffering the coin. "You send for him."

Fag pocketed the coin, produced two pennies and whispered in the ear of a man wearing a dirty red neckcloth. The man took the pennies and departed.

Returning, Tom Fag said: "Be there any other person?"

"There is," said Justice, smiling, "but I am happy to say I can find him for nothing, for I see he sits at a table yonder."

" 'Appy to oblige, gents," muttered Fag, shambling off to take further orders from his customers.

Justice pointed to a table in the shadows occupied by a slim, thin-faced man dressed rather more neatly than the tavern's usual habitués. "Useful fellow," said Justice in Bellamy's ear. "A servant in one of London's most fashionable houses. His business here? Selling information about gentlemen's houses to those who would break them open. Come."

They moved over to the table and took seats at it. The man half rose, startled, but then recognized Justice and sat down again.

"I should like to introduce you to my friend," said Justice. Then, turning to Bellamy: "This gentleman prefers to be known hereabouts simply as Jack. Jack, you are in good company, for my friend, like yourself, is of a somewhat secretive nature, and wishes to be known only as John. Or Mr. John if you prefer it. And Jack, I think you may be able to assist Mr. John."

"Oh?"

"Yes. I'm sure he would like to ask you a few questions."

"Oh!"

Bellamy produced a silver coin and laid it beside him on the table.

"Your friend, sir," said Jack. "He doesn't appear the kind to—er, he doesn't want to——?"

"Break into houses, Jack?" said the man from France. "Not physically, only with my mind. I do not want to steal gold, Jack. Only information."

36

"What do you want to know?" The question was asked cautiously.

"Where are you employed, Jack?"

"In the house of a gentleman at Wimbledon."

"What I want to know is this—are any of your friends employed in the houses of the great?"

Jack eyed the coin on the table and nodded vigorously. "That they are, sir, for in Wimbledon they are all gentlemen of means with splendid houses. There's one a member of the Parliament, another a gentleman at the foreign office——"

"Are there any living near to you who hold office at the Admiralty?"

"Strange that you ask. There's a gentleman who holds high office at the Admiralty. He don't go to sea now."

"And what of gentlemen who still go to sea, captains of fighting ships, eh?"

"I can help you there, too, sir. Why, there's a sea-farin' gent keeps a house at Merton, sir, and that is a village quite near to Wimbledon."

"Do you know his name?"

"Can't just bring it to mind," parried Jack cautiously. "Not much at home, he ain't. Most always at sea."

"Is it Admiral Collingwood?"

"No, sir."

"Admiral George Campbell?"

"No." Somehow Jack was loath to give the name.

"Well, then, Captain Thomas Hardy, of Admiral Nelson's flagship?"

"Not him."

"Admiral Nelson himself then?"

"I do believe it is." Jack's eyes fell again to the coin on the table. "Aye, the house at Merton is his."

Bellamy pushed the coin towards Jack. "Well, I didn't think the great Nelson would live near to you, Mr. Jack. But pray give him his proper title—Admiral Lord Nelson, recently promoted Vice-Admiral of the White, formerly

Vice-Admiral of the Blue, this long year and more commander-in-chief in the Mediterranean."

"You know him, sir? They say he's England's greatest sailor."

"You are quite right. He is a great sailor. But no, I do not know him."

"Then you know a deal about him."

"Let us say that I know something of—military matters," Bellamy allowed. "But let us to business. Who lives in this house at Merton when the admiral is not to home?"

Charles Justice provided the answer. "Lady Hamilton —his mistress."

Bellamy took another coin from his pocket. "It is possible we might get some of the information we want from *that* house," he observed. "Mr. Jack, have you a friend in service at that house?"

"I have."

"Do you think you could get that person to help us— just with a little information, all nice and secret and paid for?"

" 'Twould be as easy as shelling peas, Mr. John."

Bellamy flicked the coin across the table. "Then this crown piece is yours, Mr. Jack, and there will be more of them to follow. Now please to leave me, for I would not have you seen with me overlong, and meet me at six of the clock tomorrow in a different tavern. Where say you, Justice?"

"The *Surrey Stingo*."

"The *Surrey Stingo* it is, sir. Six o' the clock."

The serving man from Wimbledon left the hostelry, gripped the two crown-pieces in his pocket and smiled exultantly.

"Who is this Gentleman Jerry for whom we wait?" asked Bellamy when they were alone.

"He is a highway robber of my acquaintance," replied Justice. "He is also a person of some breeding who has found no other mode of living suitable to his talents. He is

38

not afraid of moving in polite society, and is acquainted with some men of rank. Do you not think he may be useful?"

Bellamy made a warning gesture, for at that moment a tall broad-shouldered individual dressed in the mode was being ushered to their table.

The introductions over, the three fell into a cautious conversation, until Justice said to the highwayman: "Pray do not think my friend is from the Bow Street Office or any other such inquisitive place. On the contrary, the Runners would be most happy to get their hands on him and put him safe under lock and key."

The highwayman smiled. "I had not thought he would be a thief-taker if he were a friend of yours," he said to Justice. "But it was well to make sure. Gentlemen, I am at your service."

"And I am prepared to pay for your service," said Bellamy.

"Like Mr. Justice has—in the past," returned the highwayman, whose name, it appeared, was Jeremiah Bickershaw.

"Precisely, though presumably Mr. Justice has only asked for information, while I might ask also—for action."

"What *kind* of action, pray?"

"The halting of a coach, say, on a lonely road?"

"It could be arranged. And aught further?"

"Maybe, Mr. Bickershaw. But let us not become too serious on a first meeting. Let us talk of the ladies. What can be done in that direction?"

"Ah, yes, the ladies." Bickershaw winked. "Now you would ask me to find a lady so that you may have your sport of her. Is that it, eh?"

"Tut, man, you put it most plainly. And why not, eh? A man who has the stomach to bed 'em—why, he should also have the stomach to say so."

A further meeting was arranged, and when the highwayman had taken his leave the man who had lately come from France voiced a confidence.

"I think that there I have the right sort of fellow," he

said. "He may even pull the trigger for me, if it be necessary."

Justice maintained a thoughtful silence until they were once more in the darkened streets. "I am most curious," he said to his fellow conspirator. "Can you not tell me who are they whom you have to kill? Are they politicians, soldiers or English spies. Indeed, do they include the King of England?"

"Not poor King George! That at least I can tell you. *He* cannot do France any harm." Bellamy's voice was light, but it hardened as they paced quickly from Whitefriars. "I shall tell you when I think fit," he snapped. "Until then—do me the favour of keeping silent on the matter."

CHAPTER FIVE

ON A spring morning some two dozen years before Sir Robert Peel was to found his body of police, Josiah Day came to Bow Street to organize the forces of law against London's highwaymen. He came riding in a blue coat and scarlet waistcoat—the first English policeman ever to wear uniform.

"Come to me when you have acquired a uniform you deem suitable for a cavalry peace force," Sir Richard Ford had told him. "I would suggest dark blue—a serviceable colour if public monies are to pay for it—but I leave the details to you."

So it was that Mr. Day rode bravely to the police office to be sworn as "conductor of a horse patrol". His metal buttons gleamed yellow, his sabre belt was polished till it shone and his white leather gauntlets reflected the morning sunlight.

It was as though this proud man, sent home from the Napoleonic wars with a lame leg, were once more a cavalry commander.

His spurs clinked as he came to attention before the famous magistrate, who did him the honour of rising from his desk to acknowledge his smart salute.

"You are excellently turned out, Mr. Day," said Sir Richard. " 'Tis a good uniform, and I approve of it. Let us hope it will be one to become well-known—and feared—by those who terrorize our roads.

"And now to business. As yet you have not one rider under your command, but I have this day received lists from some cavalry regiments of those who have recently left the service. You can make a start choosing from among these fellows. But first, Mr. Day, we will have you sworn."

One of the witnesses of the conductor's oath was a man with whom he was to have much in common in the months ahead, both as friend and colleague—Harry Adkins, the clever thief-catcher who had taken him before Sir Richard and made his new post possible. His eyes met those of the detective as he took the bible in one hand, raised the other and repeated these words after Sir Richard: "I accept the office under the chief magistrate's authority of constable for Middlesex, Surrey, Kent and Essex, which roads I shall have patrolled against all thieves and vagabonds and such like undesirable persons, and I swear that I shall work diligently to keep the said roads safe and peaceful for those who travel upon them."

The magistrate offered his snuff-box. "I leave you to form your patrol and take full charge of it, Mr. Day. Now for the present I will take my leave of you, for in my court a number of cut-throats and miscreants await their trial—and I must not keep them waiting.

"I wager you will soon place before me for trial a number of those damned elusive highway robbers. Mr. Day, I welcome the work you now set out to accomplish. I leave it entirely in your hands, but I shall be available at all times should you wish to consult me."

"Thank you, Sir Richard, and I pray I shall not fail you. But if I may delay you a moment longer, there is a favour I would ask. Until now I have been a cavalry officer. I shall command your new force in good discipline, but I have no knowledge of detecting criminals. Might I have some instruction from your Mr. Adkins, who I am told is an expert in such matters?"

The magistrate beckoned to the detective they called The Little Ferret. "Mr. Adkins, if you have no urgent business in hand, perhaps you would talk with Mr. Day. He is anxious, as you have just heard, to know how we run thieves to earth. You have just heard him sworn, so if you should wish to spend some time with him, and impart some of our secrets, I am sure he will be the better for your company."

"Happy to oblige." The detective led to a corner of the office and placed a second chair beside his desk. "If you will step this way, Mr. Day," he said amiably.

"First, Mr. Adkins, I should like to thank you," began the new peace officer when they were seated. "I should never have been chosen had you not put in a kind word in the beak's ear."

"Tut, sir, think nothing of it," smiled Adkins. "We were looking for a man—and I did think you the right one. Now how can I help you?"

Day took off his white gauntlets and placed them on the desk. "Well, sir, till now I have been a soldier, and I know nothing of how Ford's People, as I understand you are sometimes named, go about their business."

As he replied, the thief-taker smiled so broadly that Day decided instantly that he was a most agreeable fellow and one not at all deserving of the odium with which the peace officers were held by the public. "It is not a game with many fixed rules, and it is not, therefore, an easy one. I do think of it as a game, Mr. Day, and to me, a most absorbing one."

"As it will be to me, Mr. Adkins—as it will surely be to me. I have, as you know, suffered in the extreme at the hand of a highway rogue. Now how do you point your finger at a thief or murderer, do you not see the crime committed?"

"Well, sir, when there is a robbery or murder, myself or one of the other Runners visits the scene of the crime and ferrets out all details surrounding it. We ask many questions. Who may have been in the neighbourhood at the time? Has anyone seen any suspicious person in the vicinity?

"Sometimes the magistrate himself goes to the scene of the crime and makes his own inquiries. More often nowadays he leaves it to the Runners.

"If the thief has been seen we put a description of him in the *Covent Garden Journal* or the *Advertiser*. We list also in those journals descriptions of the goods stolen, in the hope that the pawnbrokers will remember he who brought in the goods.

"We also make use of our own police journal, the *Hue and Cry*, in which we give accounts of crimes committed, descriptions of goods stolen and of suspected thieves, and we offer rewards for any who can acquaint us with information which proves valuable, though we have to be wary of those who give false information in order to secure the reward."

"I shall be able to use that journal?"

"You will and it may help catch some highway robbers for you. But far and above such assistance, I think you will find that the greatest help to you and your men, when you get them, will be that you all keep your eyes and ears wide open."

"I shall remember it. By the way, my friend, is there any part of the city where highwaymen do congregate?"

"Aye, there is. Whitefriars is infested with 'em, as with other rogues. That is where they run with their trinkets when they have plundered the coaches."

The horse patrol officer was reaching for his gloves. "Can you take me to Whitefriars?" he asked. "Can you show me the public places they may haunt?"

The Runner rose to his feet. "I can," he said, "for I am no stranger to such places. I am at your service. When would you wish to go there?"

"I would wish to go now."

"Very well, my friend. But not in that uniform. I shall positively not take you looking so brave. 'Tis a place where a man may have his throat slit merely for looking honest."

The Runner glanced down at his own dapper civilian suit, the tan, tailed jacket, short yellow waistcoat and long, pale, tapered trousers caught up in the instep. "Neither would I go in these clothes," he said, fingering his huge, silk bow, "for they are too respectable by half for the dens of Whitefriars. However, I have some rather different suits. Ugh! Disreputable they are. I keep them in my dressing-up cupboard for jaunts of this very kind. I shall lend you one, and we shall lurk in Whitefriar's shadows with not an eyebrow raised."

Soon the two were suitably attired in soiled and scuffed

44

garments and making their way on foot towards Whitefriars. When they reached it they threaded their way through narrow streets and alleys pervaded by a permanent stench from garbage and emptied chamber pots, and Day twisted his mouth at the disagreeable surroundings. They traversed shadowed passages where the sun never reached, dim-lit areas where one could imagine the foulest crimes lying undiscovered and unnoticed from one year's end to the next.

"Makes me shudder a little," admitted Day. "I hope your duties do not bring you here too often."

"Oh, I have to come from time to time, though not for my health, as you'll agree. I have some excellent contacts in this cesspit, thieves and rogues themselves but also touts and tale-bearers. I could not do my work else. You should bless your luck, Mr. Day, that most of your work will be clerking in Bow Street or riding the open road with a wind on the heath on the darkest day."

The patrol officer's regard increased for the perky-faced, twinkling-eyed little figure stepping confidently at his side. Courage, he realized, was not a quality reserved for a cavalry charge in the face of enemy guns.

"I may have to chase some of my own rats into this sewer," he said.

"If you don't get them before they reach here," replied Adkins, "then I don't think there would be much chasing. Tracing or discovering might be better words, and I'm at your service, for I know the place. We will no doubt have to work together."

"Thank you, my friend," said Day, placing a hand on the smaller man's shoulder. "I shall have need of your help."

Adkins found his way unerringly in the maze of streets as they visited the unsavoury taverns tucked away in the darkest corners. As they sipped ale in one of them, he confided to his companion in low tones that the landlord's name was Fag. "Ought to have been taken years ago," he whispered, as the subject of their discussion shambled over to a table near to them.

"Perkin' up a bit, eh, Gentleman Jerry?" The landlord addressed its occupant with a knowing wink, and the policeman's eyes moved from the landlord to a tall, powerfully built individual with a round, red face and a scar on the left cheek that might have been an old sabre cut. He appeared to be recovering from a drunken stupor. He wore a civilian greatcoat with military frogging and an expensive but soiled cravat. He had raised his head from his folded arms, which rested on the table, and as he did so the visitors from Bow Street noted the gleam of a spur on a booted foot.

"What'll it be, Jerry, a tot o' geneva, eh?" persisted the landlord.

"Keep your perishin' gin," replied the big man, hauling himself to his feet and stretching lazily. "Just off, I am, to a better place than yours. The *Surrey Stingo*. I've an appointment there with some gentlemen friends, so out o' my way, Fag, me boy-o."

When the man referred to as Gentleman Jerry had lumbered out Adkins put a hand on Day's sleeve. "Might be interesting to follow on to the *Surrey Stingo*," he whispered.

Outside he added: "I know this character Jerry. Second name Bickershaw. Suspected in the past of breaking open some gentlemen's houses. Never had enough evidence. If they now call him *Gentleman* Jerry, I'd say he's moved up in his trade by acquiring a horse and chasing coaches on the high road."

"Ah! May be a future customer o' mine."

"May be so—if your men have their wits about them. As you see, he's got the strength of an ox, and he's a pretty desperate character to boot, though they say he's of a respectable family. I believe he'd blow your head off with a pistol as soon as look at you."

Later the two paused at the narrow doorway of the tavern they were seeking. The place had been neither washed nor painted for years, and dust and weather had obliterated the name *Surrey* over the entrance, but the word *Stingo* could be read with difficulty.

Stepping inside, Adkins looked closely about him in the dim and smoky room, where oil lanterns had to burn even in daylight. At a table in a corner he saw the man he sought, the big fellow they had followed. With him were two others, Justice and Bellamy.

Adkins did not know either, but he was aware of a rising curiosity as to why such as they should linger in Whitefriars. He sensed rather than saw that both had an air about them that was not quite in accord with their squalid surroundings. It was not their attire, for like their two observers they were clad in inconspicuous clothes; rather it was the confident manner in which they wore them.

There was no vacant table near to the trio, so the Runner and the patrol officer had to take one at the other side of the room. Soon Adkins found his interest drawn towards Justice. Was there something familiar about the man as he bent his head in what appeared to be clandestine conversation? It was difficult to decide in such a dim-lit place.

Eventually, the landlord, thinking to do the conspirators a favour, placed a lit candle on their table, and shambled off without a word. Justice's hand darted forward and snipped out the flame. But momentarily his face was illuminated, and in the single gleam it meant something to the watching detective.

"Could swear I ought to know that face," he muttered. He tried to tap memory into his forehead. "Seen it somewhere. Now damme, where was it?"

"I do not like the face," said Day, quietly.

"Nor do I. It makes me uneasy, and I do not know why. Damme if I don't make an attempt to listen to the voice." Adkins placed a hand on Day's arm. "Stay here," he said, and rising to his feet feigned a drunken walk towards the table that held their attention. Just short of it, he lowered himself heavily into a vacant chair at a table occupied by two men wearing seamen's jerseys.

47

" 'Ave a drink, mate," he leered thickly, clapping one on the shoulder. "Go on, 'ave a drink fer old time's sake."

"Don't know yer," the seaman replied, suspiciously.

" 'Course yer do," said Adkins, dribbling saliva. "We wus shipmates. 'Course yer remember. Shipmates we wus."

"Wot ship were it?" demanded the seaman.

But Adkins avoided further explanation by laying his arms on the table and drunkenly flopping his head on them.

"Puddled 'e is," decided one seaman.

"*And* barmy," agreed the other.

But they were amiable enough to leave him in his stupe-fied pose, and he strained his ears for any snatch of conversa-tion he could overhear from the next table. The words that reached him were disjointed, for they were spoken in the lowest tones. He did not recognize any voice, but the phrases that drifted over to him were most intriguing. *"Lady Hamilton . . . see where coach goes . . . don't stop it . . . follow at a distance . . . don't demand money . . . money in it for you . . . if you have her watched."*

He was prevented from hearing more, for the two seamen were rousing him, shouting for the landlord and preparing to be friendly in a boisterous manner.

"Wot ship?" persisted one of them.

"Never mind wot ship," said Adkins, slurring his words. "Yer name's Merryman, ain't it? Joe Merryman?"

"It ain't."

"Ain't it?" Bewilderment spread on the thief-taker's face.

"No, it ain't."

"Beggin' yer pardon, then." Adkins rose to his feet. "Must 'ave been mistaken. No offence, mate. Could 'ave sworn——"

Somewhat waveringly he retraced his steps, regained his seat beside Day and rested his head on his hands again.

"They're departing," hissed Day. "All three o' them—rising to go."

"Give them a minute and we'll follow," replied Adkins,

incisively. He continued to sprawl over the table, head down, simulating drunkenness, as the three passed out of the tavern. Then he was on his feet, and Day with him, making swiftly for the door.

But in the narrow lobby a drunken brawl was in progress between an unruly gang entering and one going out, and their way was blocked.

They were delayed just too long before they could shoulder their way through, and when they gained the street the three men had vanished. There were three side streets nearby, and Adkins raced to each. But dusk was gathering over London, and there was nothing to be seen.

"To the devil with those drunken louts," swore the detective. "They've made me lose those three fascinating characters."

They fell into step and began to walk briskly for Bow Street. After a thoughtful silence Adkins spoke again. "Just shows you what a sewer this place is," he said. "All I did was to take you on a conducted tour of its taverns— and hey presto, I stumble on something that looks uncommon like a crime in the making."

"It certainly looks queer, and as yet I'm no policeman," admitted Day.

"Don't like the look o' it, not one bit I don't." Harry Adkins was thinking aloud rather than conversing. "I've just nothing to go on, but I've a helluva strong feeling there's something very important afoot. Lady Hamilton, eh? Why should they be so interested in Lady Hamilton that they want her watched? And by a character as shady as Bickershaw? It's all very mysterious."

"What will you do about it?"

"*Do?* At this moment, my friend, I have no idea in the world what to do. But do something I will. Rest assured about that." The Little Ferret paused in his strutting walk and inserted his thumbs in the armholes of his yellow waistcoat.

"One o' them I've never seen in my life," he said. "Gentleman Jerry, I know a thing or two about *him*. The third, damme if I haven't seen the face before. But where, when, on what occasion? I'll remember it in time, come hell and damnation, or my name's not Harry Adkins."

CHAPTER SIX

THE Little Ferret was not present in the *Surrey Stingo* a week later to witness yet another assignation kept by Bellamy and Justice—this time with the servant from Wimbledon known as Jack.

The French spies had arrived early for the meeting, and they spent the time ingratiating themselves with the landlord, complimenting him on his wine and treating him to several of his own stiff brandies.

"We would wish to talk business in private," said Bellamy eventually. "If you had a room where we would not be disturbed?"

"I ain't got that, good sirs," returned the simpering tavern keeper. "But there's this 'ere part wot is partitioned orf from pryin' eyes."

They peered into the shadowy corner he indicated, and saw a man and woman who at this precise moment were neglecting their drinks in order to bestow upon each other a number of advanced amorous attentions.

"It will do well, but it would appear to be occupied," observed Bellamy.

"It won't be fer long, guv-nor," replied the tavern keeper, advancing purposefully upon the couple, and returning with a wink and the words: "Spoiled their fun for 'em I 'ave. Table will be free presently, sirs."

In a few minutes he was ushering the Frenchmen to the corner table, now vacant, and accepting another brandy for his pains.

After a time the man named Jack came in. His manner was furtive, and he joined the two quickly, seeming to take refuge in their dark corner.

"You would appear to be a good businessman, Mr. Jack, for you are punctual in your habits," observed Justice.

"I try to please," said Jack, smiling wryly.

"Well, I hope you can please us now," said Bellamy. "Have you been about our business at Merton?"

"I have."

"And what have you accomplished?"

"I have formed an attachment with a person in the good lord's household. As I have said, Merton is not far from Wimbledon, and there are inns where servants gather from several of the households in the area."

"This person, he is a servant at Merton?"

"Correct, sir. He is a footman."

"H'm, a footman,'" mused Bellamy, smiling somewhat sarcastically. "A splendid fellow, no doubt, but would he be likely to have much—er, information about the lord admiral?"

"I fancy he would, sir. Would it interest you to know that he is enamoured of a female servant in the same household, that he is in the habit of bedding her whenever possible, and that this female who is accepting of his advances is my Lady Hamilton's personal maid? Do I make myself plain, sir?"

"You make yourself very plain," smiled Bellamy. "You make yourself very plain indeed. Do you know, my excellent fellow, that I may yet agree with my companion that you are a tolerable businessman. You are beginning to interest me, sir. Pray tell me more."

The man from Wimbledon took a pull at his ale and became so confident as almost to smile. "Well, it would appear that every time my Lady Hamilton receives a letter from her good lord at sea she puts a flower in her hair as if to tell all the world of it. The footman of whom I speak knows of this—indeed the whole household does."

"What good is that to us, for I think the whole world knows of the affair between the admiral and the lady?" said Justice.

"But hear me out," protested Jack. "When my Lady Hamilton gets his letters it is more than she can bear but to read them out to her maid."

"Ah!" Bellamy leaned forward involuntarily.

"So you take my meaning, eh?" Jack threw a triumphant glance at Justice. " 'Tis true the whole world do know what is a-going on between the lord and his lady, but only my friend is aware that the maid knows what has been writ by my lord's hand, and by the flower in the hair he knows precisely when a letter has been received."

Bellamy rapped a knuckle on the table. "Well, come on man," he said, impatiently. "Has the footman told you the content of any of these letters?"

"That he will not do."

"Why not? Is he an old retainer? Is he loyal to the household?"

"I do not think so. He has but recently joined the household. But he is a businessman—if you get my meaning, sir."

"I do," said Bellamy. "To put it plainly, he has an itching palm and would extend it in order for it to be filled with gold meggs. I do not doubt he will get them, if he has aught to sell. When did he join the household?"

"But a few weeks ago."

"Then by my faith he's a fast worker. An eye for the ladies' charms, and he don't dally about. Bit of a whore-monger, eh? He don't believe in going without feminine comforts, eh?"

Jack, who was somewhat plain of countenance, smiled a little wickedly, then scowled. "He's as handsome as maybe," he sighed. "It do help a fellow to get his way o' the wenches."

"I'd say you were right, Mr. Jack," said Bellamy, quickly. "But we are not here to discuss strumpets and their wares. What is the next move in our game with your fornicating footman?"

"He's willing to meet you, but not here. He says you must come to him. You must meet him a few miles from Wimbledon in the *Green Man* at Putney. I can arrange it easy as falling off a horse, and I'd suggest you bring your purse with you. Will you come?"

Bellamy wore a satisfied grin. "We will come," he said.

"I do not like it." The words were delivered by Harry Adkins as a considered opinion. What he had overheard in the *Surrey Stingo* had continued to fascinate him. The few words that had drifted to his ears meant little by themselves, but he was concerned that in such a district Lady Hamilton's name should be whispered behind a secretive hand. And eventually he had decided to report the matter to Sir Richard Ford.

"I confess I do not know what to make of it," said the magistrate. "Have you any supposition to put forward, Mr. Adkins?"

The Runner tapped his forehead. "Maybe they were plotting to break open the lady's house—or rather I should say Lord Nelson's house, for in reality it is his, though it is she who makes her home there. Possibly the scoundrels plan to break it open during the admiral's absence at sea."

"Possibly."

"Yet why should they want her watched when she takes a journey by coach? Do they want to study her habits, so as to know the best time to break into the house? I do not know why, but I have a strange sense that we have stumbled on something of uncommon importance."

"Of more importance, do you think, than common crime? What is in your mind, Mr. Adkins?"

"I do not know. I cannot even hazard a guess. But at the back of my mind is the fact that she is Admiral Nelson's mistress, and Admiral Nelson is a man of uncommon importance. A mistress is always a dangerous commodity, the more so for any such as he. I do think, Sir Richard, that gentlemen of such renown would do better not to take a mistress at all."

"You do, eh?" Sir Richard moved in his chair, and his quill dropped from his hand. The click and rattle it made on the desk was followed by a strained silence in which the detective remembered that the magistrate himself had in the past lived openly with a mistress, the celebrated actress, Mrs. Dorothy Jordan, who with his consent had styled herself "Mrs. Ford".

"I think in the case of the admiral it does not do him well," declared the detective.

"H'm, yet he is truly idolized. England has never had an admiral who was better loved."

"Such sentiments as I express about women are due no doubt to my lack of adventures with them. I have neither married nor kept a mistress."

"Off with you, my good Adkins. Are you so puritanical?"

Adkins smiled. "Either that, Sir Richard, or I cannot afford such pleasures."

"Wait till you meet a woman you cannot resist," said the magistrate, in the most genial tones. "You will make yourself afford it—or mope around for the rest of your days."

"I will take your word for it," returned Adkins. "But in the meantime, I am more worried that some scoundrels from Whitefriars are much too interested in my Lady Hamilton. I think with your permission I will at least make a call upon the lady and warn her there may be a plot to break open her home."

"Do whatever you think fit, Mr. Adkins. You know that my rat catchers—and you in particular—are allowed a free hand, all eight of you, and that you detect and apprehend thieves and vagabonds in your own time and in your own way."

"I'll get me to Merton at once, then," replied Adkins.

The thief-taker, this smiling, dapper fellow in civilian clothes, whose cleverness appeared always to be hidden by lethargic movements and an ambling gait, passed on his way out of the office a desk at which Mr. Day was engaged in working out something foreign to the little Runner and his way of working. Chewing the end of his quill, the conductor was drawing up a comprehensive form of discipline for his horse patrol.

Adkins paused to bend over the uniformed figure. "I'm about to make a call on Lady Hamilton," he drawled, "and one never knows what intelligence I may pick up."

The footman who worked at Merton Place stood in the *Green Man* on the fringe of Putney Heath gripping the handle of his tankard with one hand and drumming impatiently on the bar counter with the fingers of the other. His name was Jedd Stickles, and he was a tall, even-featured individual with dark, brilliant eyes and a long, thin, carefully trimmed moustache that appeared to have been painted on his upper lip.

He held his tankard with two of his fingers raised daintily, and made gracious and studied gestures which he had copied from those whom people somewhat exasperatingly termed "his betters". Indeed, in his spotless, white hose and long-coated livery he cut quite the figure of a gentleman —until he spoke. For not to leave anything undone, the practised imitator had developed *A Voice* and *A Speech* which fell quaintly short of that which he wished to affect.

The two he was to meet, he decided, would have to pay well for any information he was to supply. It was not, as it transpired, altogether convenient to be waiting on these strangers, for not two hours ago Lady Hamilton had dismissed her maid for the evening, and at this precise moment Jedd Stickles could have been in her arms and in her bed. However, there was the question of money, a commodity he found as agreeable as his sultry, raven-haired temptress.

At last the three for whom he waited entered the little inn parlour, and he addressed the one he knew.

"I h'am of the opinion, Jumper, that you h'are somewhat late," said Stickles loftily and in his affected voice. "I thought you was never coming, that I did."

Justice snapped his fingers triumphantly in the face of the man he knew as Jack. "It would appear we are now in possession of your name. I take it Jumper is your surname, unless it be a nickname to confuse the issue still further?"

"It is my surname."

"An honest name enough, my fellow," said Bellamy. "Why so shy about it?"

"I do not bandy it about in the place where I met you, but I am rather better known in these parts."

"What a mysterious fellow you are. One would think every peace officer in London were after you. However, I suppose you know your own business best. Jack, then, is your given name?"

"It is."

"Jack Jumper. I shall remember the name, but I promise not to bandy it about if it so pleases you. I'd say one of your ancestors could leap prodigiously well, or was in the habit of jumping prison. A good, respectable nickname, once upon a time, eh? Now to business. So this is your friend, and has he a name that can be divulged, or must it be whispered beneath the folds of a dark cloak?"

The reply came quickly from the man to whom the Frenchman referred. He drew himself to the full height of his six feet two inches and declared: "Jedd Stickles, h'esquire. That's my name, and I'd tell it to the King hisself, h'if he was to present hisself this minute."

"Excellent!" Bellamy smiled and half-bowed. "Jumper, my good fellow, pray present us to Mr. Stickles."

The introductions completed, Stickles came to the point with an alarming lack of finesse. "Well, wot do you desire of me, pray? Come, sirs, I h'ain't got all night, being h'as how I have other pleasures to my taste."

"Quite," put in Justice, grinning.

"So h'if you will h'acquaint me of your requirements I will do my best to h'accede," said Stickles pompously, "always supposin' the payment is of a satisfactory nature."

"Pray hold a moment, Mr. Stickles," said Bellamy, in a low voice. "You are too bold by half to wish to speak in a public place so near to where you are known. If you are to be of use to me you must be cautious, and have your wits

57

about you. In this tavern we shall take a little refreshment, that is all. I have a coach outside where we can talk, with no ears wagging."

"I beg pardon, sir." Stickles the boastful was already conquered by Bellamy's personality.

"Then hold your tongue and take wine with me."

Later, a few paces from the tavern, the four stood in the dark near a coach drawn up at the edge of Putney Heath, and Bellamy addressed the man who had brought them there. "Mr. Jumper, you have despatched your work well for one night. You may ride with us to Wimbledon, and may alight near to the house where you are employed."

The four settled themselves in the coach and Stickles saw a large silver coin change hands and noted Jumper's smile of satisfaction.

As the coach began to lumber along the road through the heath the lighted windows of a solitary building were visible through the trees.

"I gather, beggin' your pardon, sirs, that it's matters appertaining to the h'Admirallity you be interested in?" volunteered Jumper. "If it's of interest, sirs, the place you see yonder is an inn by the name o' *The Telegraph*."

"I have heard of the place," returned Justice. "A signal post, is it not?"

"You could call it that," replied Jumper. "There's a line o' posts spaced out all the way from Portsmouth which sends on messages to London. This be the last in the link, for from its roof signals can be exchanged with the Admirallity in the city, by flag during the day and by lamp at night, be it not a time o' fog or mist."

Bellamy glanced at Justice. "Remember the fact, Charles," he ordered. "It might be useful. And Jumper, do you know folk in the *Telegraph Inn*?"

"They know me there," came the reply. "Landlord keeps a good jug o' ale."

"Perhaps you would be good enough to find out all you can about the place, eh?"

"I will—and if you will drop me off here, Mr. Bellamy——"

"Are we at the house?"

"We ain't. But 'tis a short walk, and I'd rather you did not know precisely the spot. I'd prefer you didn't ever call upon me there."

"You must learn to trust us," said Justice.

"Aye," said Jumper, drily.

As he alighted, Bellamy said: "One thing more, my friend. Remember saying a gentleman from the Admiralty kept a house hereabouts? Be a good fellow and find out more about him."

"When do we meet again?" countered Jumper.

"Sunday, eight of the clock in the evening. The *Surrey Stingo.*"

"Eight of the clock it is, sir." With the words Jack Jumper vanished, whistling cheerfully, into the darkness. As he did so he was surprised to see a horseman, his face and form indistinguishable in the night, following the coach at a discreet distance. The rider hailed him, as a stranger might, wishing him a good night, and Jumper fancied he recognized the voice. He stood for a moment staring after the shadowy horseman and the disappearing coach. Then he shrugged his shoulders and turned for home.

When Jack Jumper had gone he appeared to have taken with him some of Jedd Stickles's boldness. The man from Merton sat very silent for a time, gazing through the window at the flying trees.

"And now to *our* business, Mr. Stickles," began Bellamy.

"Er, yes."

"Now I understand that you can acquaint yourself with the text of my Lord Nelson's letters of the heart penned from sea to my Lady Hamilton."

"Don't know as I should acquaint strangers h'of such matters. Don't know who you h'are."

"Come, Mr. Stickles. Of course you do. Has not your

59

good friend presented us properly? Should you have forgot, I am John Bellamy. This is Charles Justice."

"But who *are* you?"

"My friend has just told you," said Justice grimly.

"Oh! I mean, why should you want h'information about milady's letters? I h'am not so sure now that I should have met you—h'or entered this coach."

"That is precisely what we thought would occur to you when we came, for you were reluctant to meet us on our own ground. But you are quite safe *provided you are a sensible fellow.*"

"I don't know as I should——"

"Pray be silent for a moment," rapped Bellamy. "Listen to my words, for I think you protest too much. I am by way of being a professor of the written word, a student of human nature, and I am writing a lengthy treatise on love and the making of love. My friend, who is also a learned gentleman, is assisting me. 'Tis not a criminal offence, eh? You yourself are not averse to the charms of the fair sex, eh? Besides, there's money in it for you."

"Is that why you went to Whitefriars, to that den?"

"Precisely. I cannot be a student of human nature and stay only among the quality." Bellamy produced a crown piece and twirled it between finger and thumb. "This is for you, if you are a good fellow."

"I don't know——"

"Is it not enough?"

"It's enough." Stickles was wide-eyed. There was something, he felt, not quite as it should be with the other occupants of the coach, but he could not place a finger on what it was. It was all right Jack Jumper mixing with strange characters in Whitefriars, but he, Jedd Stickles, was more discerning. "But I want no part in it," he continued, leaning forward as if he would rise to his feet. "Let me out of this coach."

"Stop the coach, Charles," ordered Bellamy.

"Stop the coach," roared Justice, thrusting his head out of the window.

The driver was hauling on the reins and the coach was creaking and crunching to a halt.

It was the pre-arranged signal for the horseman who followed to act, but only the two Frenchmen knew it. Gentleman Jerry Bickershaw, for it was he who rode behind, spurred forward.

Two pistols appeared through the window, then a tall, black hat and a masked face. Jedd Stickles received a fright from which he was not likely to recover quickly.

He leaned back in his seat, as far away from the pistols as possible, more alarmed by far with them than the conversation that had ensued before. In his fear, he failed to realize that the coachman had not challenged the highwayman, who in his turn had ignored the possibility of a blunderbuss being discharged on him from above. Which was not at all surprising, for he who handled the horses aloft was a certain young Mr. Swift, a fellow conspirator of Bellamy and one of those who had met him on the beach when he had arrived from France.

"So, gentlemen, you would halt your coach on *my* heath. You are much too brave, my fine fellows, for I'm the King o' the Portsmouth Road, or at least the bit that runs o'er this common."

"I do not like your tone," said Bellamy, knowing that he spoke in perfect safety.

"Bravo, my hearty," returned the highwayman. "But are you all so daring? What of you, sir?" He turned his attention to Stickles, leaning forward and prodding him in the chest with the muzzle of a pistol. "How'd you like to die, eh? It'd be as easy as mounting a horse. I just have to press on the trigger, and bang—you'd be as dead as a mutton cutlet."

The servant from Merton sat as still as if he were already dead, mesmerized, his face ashen.

"I'll relieve you of any money you have about your person," continued Gentleman Jerry, prodding Stickles in the chest with a pistol. "Quickly now, and if it's not enough to please me I'll castrate you, that I will."

Stickles was speechless, terror-stricken. He appeared also to be paralysed, for he could not move his hand.

Suddenly Bellamy acted, again quite safely. "Look behind you, Mr. Highway Robber," he said. "There is a rapier pointing to your back."

As the masked head turned, Bellamy wrenched both pistols from the man's hands, as had been arranged. "Now get you gone, sirrah," he roared, pointing the weapons at the highwayman, "and leave us in peace to our talks."

Gentleman Jerry turned his horse's head and clattered away into the darkness.

Stickles's gratitude to Bellamy knew no bounds. "I—I thank you, sir," he gasped. "I do thank you."

" 'Twas nothing," said Bellamy. "Mr. Justice, have you a flask about you? A swig for Mr. Stickles. He has had a nasty experience. Thought he was going to lose his testicles."

"You saved my life, sir," said the footman, gulping from the flask. "And my money, though I doubt if what I have about me would have satisfied that ruffian."

"Ah, talking of money—not only have I saved some for you. Why, I am at pains to give you more, do you agree to help me in my work."

"I do agree. You are a splendid gentleman, sir."

Bellamy was the soul of geniality. "So, there are worse things than helping a philosopher to pen his treatise? You will be safe in my company. Never forget it. Take this crown-piece now. It should help you to recover your wits."

The footman took the coin.

"As I was saying before, your friend, Mr. Jumper, tells me you know much of what the admiral writes to his lady," said Bellamy, studying his finger nails.

"I don't never read what I'm not supposed to. I am no sneak in the night."

"I did not say you were. Nor should I be interested. Please to tell me what you know of the letters."

62

"They all begin, 'My dearest Emma'. They tell of his love and how he misses her—Lady Hamilton, I mean."

"Does he write, in these letters, aught of his affairs at sea?"

"He does. He writes freely of them."

"For example?"

The servant from Merton settled himself more comfortably in the coach seat and pocketed the coin. "My lady's maid has told me what has been writ, even back to months before I came to Merton. She has h'an excellent mem'ry. No less do I. I can tell you much of Admiral Nelson's movements since the turn o' the year. The year was a fortnight old when the French Admiral Villeneuve left Toulon with a fleet o' ships.

"My Lord Nelson wrote that this caused him more anxiety than aught for seven years. Chased him he did wi' his own ships, but lorst him. Again he wrote to tell Lady Hamilton that h'a month later—the 19th day o' February it was—he heard that Villeneuve had returned to Toulon. Now Villeneuve has left port again, h'and Nelson, with twelve ships o' the line, h'is chasing him."

"Excellent! You have a fine memory, and it pleases me well." Bellamy took another coin from his pocket and in the pale night it flashed silver. "It would appear you would be one of the first to know when and if the good admiral is returning home?"

"Reckon Lady Hamilton would be the first—and me not long after."

"Good." Bellamy proffered the coin. "You and your lady friend, remember if you please every detail in each letter that now comes from the admiral. Mr. Justice, please to tell the coachman to proceed to Merton, and we will set Mr. Stickles at his doorstep—safe and sound from highway robbers."

When they had left the servant, young Swift turned the coach about, whipped up the horses and rattled for London at a round pace. Inside, the two French spies lay back on the seats and relaxed in the jolting, swaying vehicle.

There was a long silence, broken by Justice. *"Sacré bleu, mon ami,"* he said. "How much would you wager that I have now guessed the precise nature of your mission in England?"

"I would not wager anything, Charles," came the reply. "I think you may well have guessed, but you had to know in time, and I have now decided that I trust you."

"You are here," suggested Justice, in a low, strained voice that held a note of pure excitement, "to assassinate the famous admiral."

"The man of whom you speak," said Bellamy, "is a thorn in the flesh of our Napoleon Bonaparte. Give the sailor his due, he is an inspired naval commander whom England could not lightly spare. He has the imagination of six admirals, and he is so loved that every sailor in the British Navy would follow him into hell.

"As a fighting man myself, I hold this Horatio Nelson in the highest esteem, and I am hating the task I have been set as I have never hated another thing in all my life. Perhaps that is why I have been chosen, for a man who feels deeply will do his task well.

"It must be done, this thing I have to do, for our invasion flotillas have to cross that sea in safety, and Bonaparte has more than a suspicion that Villeneuve actually fears this English sailor."

The officer from France paused, his eyes lowered. Then he raised his head and his eyes were flashing in the dark. "You have guessed rightly, *mon ami*," he said, very softly. "I am here to remove the Admiral Lord Nelson from the scene of our endeavours—and God rest his soul."

CHAPTER SEVEN

HARRY ADKINS went to Merton astride an old and peaceable nag, not so much because he was a calm, unhurried sort of fellow as that he was no born horseman.

But on this day he was cutting a gayer figure than usual. For his trip into the country he had exchanged his black topper for a wide-brimmed white hat and his tapering trousers for knee-breeches and gaiters. In addition, he had put on his best, pale-blue, tailed jacket—not altogether because he was to visit the famous admiral's lady, but also because he now felt he could afford to wear the resplendent garment more often as his pay had just been raised to a guinea a week.

Moreover, he was paid a guinea a day and fourteen shillings expenses by any private person or organization to whom he was loaned out by the police office. And there were plenty requiring a thief-taker's skill, including theatres, the Bank of England and the Revenue men. Even the government had in the past asked for the services of some of the eight Bow Street Runners to track down escaping prisoners-of-war before the daring little smuggling vessels could take them on a fair wind to France.

So it was that he jogged proudly if slowly on the road to Surrey. Let them call London's peace officers by odious names until they shouted themselves hoarse. For was not his income above average? Was he not recognized as one of the cleverest of the thief-takers, of whom there was but a handful in the whole of London?

When the houses began to straggle by the wayside, he sniffed the spring air with satisfaction. Was it not good to be trusted? Dignified, too. When the magistrate gave a Runner an assignment, that officer was not expected to report or explain what he was doing, or why he was doing it, until he brought in his man. He, Harry Adkins, thief-taker extraordinary, would vanish like the ferret they called him, no one caring a fig for his absence, or ever criticizing his expense account, until he emerged with something to show for his pains.

In the leafy lanes and on the open road he gave not a thought to the possibility of an encounter with a highway scoundrel. "I am the law," he always told himself, and the brief, philosophic motto, ingrained into his personality, seemed to afford him a strange measure of protection. Which on occasions he sorely needed, for he carried no weapon but a long, stout ebony cane surmounted by a heavy silver knob. He did not often handle a fire-arm, and though his courage could not be questioned—well, if the truth were known, he did not really have the stomach for them.

It was an hour past midday when he turned his horse's head into the drive at Merton and tethered the animal to a railing before handling the big brass knocker on the door.

"A good day to you," he said, cheerfully, when it swung open and a handsome, dark-eyed footman gazed at him with polite indifference. "Would be happy to know if her ladyship is to home?"

"'Fraid not, sir."

"Might I ask if she is expected home soon?"

"You might." The servant had an air of bogus superiority. "But why do you h'ask, sir?"

"I should have thought it quite obvious, my fine fellow." The flashing smile might have melted the most granite heart, but it did not mask the note of authority. "I should like to speak with her ladyship."

"Ah! I did not catch your name, sir."

"I am not surprised. I had not as yet given it. Adkins is the name. Adkins, of—er, London."

"I see," said the footman, in a tone which indicated he did not see at all. "And your business?"

"Thank you for your interest, my good man, but my business is with Lady Hamilton."

"I see," said the footman again. "Well, her ladyship may return at any time. At the minute she is out riding."

"Then I should like to wait."

"Depending on the nature of your business——"

"It is *official* business."

"Ah!"

"And I shall wait. Er, on the doorstep if necessary."

"P'raps, then, you would care to step h'inside to await her ladyship."

"I should be delighted to accept that gesture of hospitality."

The Bow Street officer was then ushered into a panelled room off the hallway. Little more than a vestibule, it contained a small table and two uncomfortable, high-backed chairs.

The footman, who had decided the visitor was neither of inferior station nor a man to be trifled with, now did him the honour of a slight, stiff bow. "If I may acquaint her ladyship where you come from?"

Possessing himself the same characteristic, the detective divined in the man an obsessive curiosity, but he matched it with his own determination to hide his true identity from tongue-wagging servants.

"Thank you, I shall acquaint her myself," he said.

He settled down to wait. On the wall above the table was an ornate, gilt mirror in which he could see his own broad forehead and pink-complexioned, clean-shaven face, his bright, questing eyes and flaxen hair that hid his ears like a wig and defied to some extent the frequent and vigorous brushings he bestowed on it. It was a pleasant, animated face, cheerful and generous if not endowed with consummate good looks.

He sat down but rose again to study two portraits side by side on the wall. One was obviously of Horatio Nelson; the set of the mouth and the thin, pale cheeks were unmistakable, and the painter had touched into the eye the gleam of dreams. The famous admiral had sat for the portrait resplendent in his long-tailed, gold-braided naval tunic, white breeches and hose and, proud, vain man that he was he had pinned to it every glittering star and honour he had won.

The painting by its side was, Adkins presumed, that of "his dearest Emma". So this was the woman he had come to see? If the portrait did her justice, it showed a dark-haired, dainty-mouthed, large-eyed face wearing an expression of child-like innocence. Well, she certainly wasn't that. No matter how well England loved her illustrious sailor, or in his turn he loved his Emma, there was nothing child-like about her association with him. It would be interesting to see if she favoured her portrait . . .

But there was to be a feminine face infinitely more interesting to him, for Lady Hamilton's was not the only one on which his eyes were to feast in the elegant drawing-room before he took his leave of Merton Place.

He was well used to waiting, this patient, painstaking man, and this time he was to be rewarded with something he had not expected. For when the footman presented him in the open doorway of the drawing-room he was conscious of two women within, and as he rose from his bow his eyes rested briefly on Lady Hamilton's face before remaining on that of her companion for a longer time than was necessary.

The one face was certainly that of Lord Nelson's "dearest Emma", the other a countenance that to the thief-taker held a strange appeal that he could not quite understand.

"Good day to you." Lady Hamilton's loud yet not disagreeable voice cut in on his thoughts. "Mr. Adkins, is it?"

"Harry Adkins, of the Bow Street Public Office, at your service, my lady."

"Oh! Have I offended the law in some way, Mr. Adkins?"

The officer's expansive smile was both friendly and reassuring. "No, my lady, not in any way. I come on a most peaceful errand."

"I am pleased at that. Will you be seated? But first, may I present Miss Rosemary Hart?"

Adkins bowed again, very low, and it was with difficulty

68

that he took his eyes from Miss Hart when he became aware that Lady Hamilton was addressing him once more. "My niece is staying with me for a short spell. Her home is in the rustic north parts, in the county of Cheshire, and I am showing her what manner of place is our London Town."

The detective felt there was something he should remark, but for once his tongue was tied.

"Well, Mr. Adkins? You may talk before my niece. Among her talents are those of trustworthiness and loyalty."

"I am—sure of it," stumbled Adkins. Forcing himself to concentrate on the reason for his visit, he went on more confidently: "The fact is, ma'am, that I have reason to believe that some thieves and vagabonds are much too interested in this house. I came to warn you of this."

"I am most obliged——"

"And to ask you some questions."

"What would you like to know, Mr. Adkins?"

The visitor stroked his chin meditatively. "To begin with, do you know any reason why any rascally character should be set to watch your coach, to ride after it and find where you go and what you do?"

"Bless me, sir, but I have no idea. 'Tis most disturbing."

"Have you any enemies, any that would do you ill?"

Lady Hamilton's smile had vanished. "There are—there must be those who tattle about me, spreading the vilest gossip about my association with my dearest Lord Nelson, but I know of none who would do me ill."

"I do not wish to alarm you. The chief magistrate at Bow Street is this minute arranging to have the roads patrolled for the safety of those who use them. In the meantime, what of your coachman? Is he trustworthy?"

"None better, Mr. Adkins."

"Then ask him to carry a blunderbuss and to keep it well primed. Now I must ask you a further question—is there aught in this house belonging to my Lord Nelson that any scoundrel would wish to get his hands on?"

"There are the things any common thief might desire—

that is all. Merton Place is but my Lord Nelson's home when he is not at sea."

"Well, it may be that some rogues would watch your movements so as to choose their best time to break open this house. But why this house in particular? Frankly, my lady, I do not know."

Lady Hamilton did not appear to be so puzzled. "It is a house which might seem to contain valuables, is it not?" she said.

"It is that kind of house, I grant you. But the conspirators were at their plotting the best part of ten miles away. No, I do not understand it. However, I advise you to see that your doors are well secured and your windows shuttered at nights. In addition, I would ask a favour of you. If anything suspicious should happen, in this household or outside of it, I ask that I be informed of it at the earliest. If such should occur, please to send urgent word to me at the public office at Bow Street."

"I shall do as you ask. I hope it will not be necessary, but I thank you for your goodness in coming here."

Adkins rose. "It is but my duty," he said. Then he stole a glance at the younger woman, who had remained silent. The shy smile she gave him confused the scientific brain, and this had never happened before . . . "I hope, Miss Hart, that you are enjoying your stay in Surrey," he found himself saying.

"I find it most agreeable," she replied, in a quiet, singing voice that he thought very attractive.

"And you are remaining some time longer?"

"I hope to do so, sir."

He wanted to ask just how long she would be staying at Merton. Instead he found himself saying: "Well, I must take my leave of you, my lady—Miss Hart."

At the door he paused and turned. "A last word, ma'am," he said. "I should not talk of this matter to any of your servants—or tell them I am an officer from Bow Street. It would be wise to do as I say."

As he returned to London, he was uncomfortably aware that he was no wiser about the strange whispered conversation he had overheard in that notorious Whitefriars ale house. His visit to the famous admiral's home had unearthed not the smallest clue to the matter, and if the scoundrels still plotted then they did so in perfect safety.

Equally disturbing was the fact that time and again his mind wandered from a professional problem he sensed to be important to a certain Miss Rosemary Hart, of whom he knew so little, save that he liked her smile, and his mind had never before gone a-roving when he had set it to work.

CHAPTER EIGHT

THE messenger had ridden hard from Wimbledon and his face was flushed and wet with rain as he strode into the Bow Street office and drew an envelope from the folds of his cloak. Taking it from him, Harry Adkins started as the man announced the district from which he had come.

The officer studied the letter carefully, the fingers of one hand drumming on the desk. This is what he read:

> *I see from your advertisements in the journals that the general publick are requested to furnish you with the fullest possible details forthwith whenever a dastardly crime hath been committed, as you do believe in quick notification and speedy pursuit.*
>
> *My house here hath been broken open by some very clever thieves, the identity of whom I have no knowledge whatsoever, and they have got clean away.*
>
> *I must confess to very little having been stolen in the way of monies or valuable objects, but the miscreant hath rummaged among all my private papers, many of which lie scattered about the house.*
>
> *Consequently, I did think that as I do hold a position of some considerable trust at the central offices of His Majesty's Admiralty in London you should be speedily informed of the said crime.*
>
> *I now leave the matter in your hands, and hope to hear from you at your earliest.*
> *I am,*
> *Yours respectfully,*
> *James Sketterhorn.*
> *First secretary to the Admiralty.*

Adkins put the letter in a pocket, rose slowly to his full

height of five feet and eight inches, puffed out his chest, inserted his thumbs in the armholes of his fancy waistcoat and gazed thoughtfully at the messenger before speaking. "Please to thank your master," he said, "and tell him I shall take charge of the investigations personally. The name is Adkins. Officer Harry Adkins. I shall visit his house, and inform him if you will that in the meantime everything should be left as it was by the thief. Pray do not tidy anything away."

Having informed the chief magistrate of the break-in, the detective put on his cloak, but paused at his friend's desk as he made for the door. "House at Wimbledon broken open, Mr. Day," he said. "Most intriguing. In the first place, it is the home of the first secretary at the Admiralty. In the second, it cannot be far from my Lady Hamilton's, where we already fear a robbery. And in the third, my lady is the mistress of my Lord Nelson. Who is so interested in admirals, eh?"

Josiah Day's pen stopped scratching. "Are you thinking of those strange fellows in the *Surrey Stingo?*" he asked. "Are you making any guesses?"

"Tut, Mr. Day, it is dangerous to guess. It tends to make the brain lazy and drowns the processes of deduction in a cloud like a London fog. One cannot guess. One has to know."

The patrol commander was smiling. "Forgive me, Mr. Adkins, for I am but a beginner," he said. "Are you riding to Wimbledon, then?"

Adkins was beginning to smile, too, very broadly. "This minute," he said, "and I have a mind to take the opportunity of calling also on my Lady Hamilton—er, to ask if there has been any attempt to rob her of late."

"You would not have another reason also, eh?" said Day, winking meaningly. "You confided that your last visit was most agreeable."

"Damme, Mr. Day, my visit will be most professional," returned the Runner, playfully, slapping his colleague on

73

the back. "I should not, I see now, have confided in you about my lady's niece."

"I fear me you would have had an apoplectic had you not. I never did see a man so moonsick."

"My good fellow, I keep you from your work—and how does it progress, by the way? I promised my Lady Hamilton that she would be kept safe by our horse patrol."

"I shall do my best to keep them unmolested—and her niece, too, while she stays within twenty miles of London." Day shuffled the papers on his desk. "I am to be allowed fifty-two troopers and one inspector, and I've enlisted already half the number. I am to begin drilling them tomorrow. My boys, by the way, are to cost £800 a year."

"Worth twice the sum if it keeps down the highway scoundrels," commented Adkins.

"I shall have them patrol the main roads in thirteen companies for twenty miles out of the city. They are to take particular notice of all persons of suspicious appearance whom they may see on the road, and to pay attention to whatever information they may receive of any highway robbery having been committed—or attempted. I know you're hell bent on getting to Wimbledon, but I'd like you to listen to these rules of discipline I've made out, for you may help me with them, and once you put your nose on a case the good Lord knows when we shall see you again."

Adkins heaved himself on to the edge of the desk. "Pray continue, my good fellow," he said, "though all this jingle of spurs is not much in my line."

"Thank you, my friend." Day began reading from his papers. "In the case of a highway robbery the patrol is to obtain a description of the robber, discover the road on which he has made off, and try to take the offender. If the party be apprehended, he is to be lodged in some place of security until he can be brought to the public office. Meanwhile, the patrol is to take the addresses of the witnesses, and warn them to attend before a justice the following morning."

74

" 'Tis much as we work, though without horses," commented Adkins.

"So I'm on the right lines. I will continue reading. Every patrol will wear his uniform, have his pistol loaded and his sabre to hand on the outside of his coat, and he is not to go off the high road or into any public house except in pursuit of the offender. I have more rules to set down, but what think you of these I have already writ?"

Adkins slid off the desk and clapped Day on the back. "I think that I made no vain promise to my Lady Hamilton," he said. "I think the time is to come when the traveller is to be made very safe."

When the Runner had gone the man with a military mind went on scratching with his quill:

No patrol while on duty is to suffer his horse to be out of his sight.

If his horse becomes unfit, he is to continue to patrol on foot.

If any patrol shall not be met by the other patrol he is to report this to me, or my inspector or one of my deputy-inspectors, and not any excuse will be admitted for failing to make such a report.

Every patrol when from home is to wear his uniform; otherwise it will be deemed he is ashamed of the situation he holds and unfit to be retained.

If it shall appear that any patrol has by unjust or disreputable conduct disgraced the situation he holds by obtaining a bad character he will forthwith be dismissed the service.

If any patrol be found drunk on duty he will be forthwith discharged.

Mr. Day, who was to well earn his starting salary of £175 a year, went on writing.

Young Mr. Speed, one of the French spy's team, was

relieved to have returned without being seen from the Admiralty official's house in Wimbledon to Justice's lodgings in a small, square court off Ludgate Hill. For ringing in his ears as he rifled Sketterhorn's bureau had been the hollow, expressionless voice of John Bellamy and his grim, unmerciful words:

"Should you be caught, you will not identify yourself with this house, with me or with our mission. Instead, you will go to the gallows as a private person and an ordinary thief, under the name you have adopted and not that with which you were baptized in France.

"To any prison chaplain who begs you to confess to your crime you will not admit to your real name, or what you do in England, but only to the crime of which you may be convicted. You might just as well do as I order. If you do not, I shall kill you with my own hands. For God bless— and make victorious—our great Napoleon Bonaparte."

But Speed had not been caught, and now he drank wine in safety with the other members of his little group.

"You are quite certain there was no mention of Admiral Nelson among the man's papers?" said Bellamy for the third time that morning.

"I am positive," replied Speed. "There was but the one bureau I could find, and I had every paper out of it. I stole two candlesticks to make it seem a robbery. Silver they were —and of a value enough to hang me."

"Did you find *anything* of use to us?"

"Yes, of use to M'sieur Justice and the work he did before you came. Information about British ships of the line and their deployment. I have committed it to memory, and will give the facts to M'sieur Justice whenever he requires them."

Bellamy paced the room. "We may in the end have to rely on young passion-breeches at Merton Place," he said. "But I'd as soon have a second source of intelligence to match with that of the sensual Mr. Stickles."

Meanwhile, Harry Adkins was examining Sketterhorn's house in some detail. He satisfied himself that an entry had been forced from outside through a window and decided that footprints on the flower beds outside it had been made by riding boots. Nothing that might help to identify the intruder had been dropped either inside or outside the building. The bureau itself had been prized open in a somewhat clumsy manner, and all the papers spilled from its various compartments.

He set Sketterhorn to studying every paper to discover if any were missing and conducted a fruitless questioning of the servants. Eventually he turned his attention to the Admiralty official himself.

"Well, sir, are any of the papers missing?"

"As far as I can see—none."

"How important are the papers?"

"Relatively important. Those that are vital are well locked and guarded at my office in the city."

"H'm, as you say two candlesticks are missing. It is rather odd, sir, for I can see several items of greater value that might have been carried away with ease. Yet they remain untouched. Do you not think that strange?"

"I am but thankful the damage is no greater."

Did the thief think the bureau had contained anything of value on account of its being locked? If none of the papers was missing, did this mean the intruder was not interested in them? Had the criminal known the house was Sketterhorn's? Or, if so, what position Sketterhorn held?

Adkins left asking himself these and other questions—and finding no satisfactory answers.

The only thing of which he was certain was what he had known before he set foot from Bow Street—that an intruder had broken into the private house of an Admiralty official.

He was finally and uncomfortably aware of this as he entered the gates of Merton Place. Why he should think this particular robbery important he did not know. It was as yet a whim born of an uncanny sixth sense with which he was gifted and that had helped to distinguish him as an investigator.

But there was a wind in the tall trees beyond the gates, and for the moment it blew the strange fancy from his head. A glimpse of the house he had visited so recently replaced it, not unnaturally in the circumstances, with thoughts totally unconnected with his duties . . .

Would she be there still, as she was on that other day, the utterly delightful Miss Hart, sitting demurely and gravely, obviously a little uncertain in such grand surroundings, like an innocent thought in an evil world?

He had judged her to be a poorer relative of this Lady Hamilton, who had been born plain Emma Hart, or some said Emma Lyon, in a rural backwater in the north parts. For had it not been said that the father of Lord Nelson's mistress had been a blacksmith in Cheshire?

There were those who might not have termed Miss Rosemary Hart a ravishing beauty. But then Harry Adkins did not share the famous admiral's belief in Emma Hamilton's looks. Nor yet those of the distinguished painters who had clamoured to reproduce her features on canvas. Life—and love—were strange and unpredictable.

The detective may have been attracted to Lady Hamilton's niece partly because of what he had sensed about her background. For was not he himself set in the same mould. Like her, he was now a most presentable person, dressed in the mode and with a cheerful and confident approach. But he was not a gentleman born. He had, however, inherited from his humble ancestors some qualities of brain and character—and a spark of that strange, intangible something that makes a man different from his neighbour. These—and hard work—had lifted him by his bootstraps beyond the station to which he had been born.

He had already demonstrated this air of superiority on the footman, a handsomer figure by far than he, and this time he was bowed in at once.

Soon he was himself bowing in the doorway of the

78

drawing-room—and yes, there she was, the delectable Miss Rosemary Hart, whom his eyes found before they rested on Lady Hamilton.

"Mr. Adkins," said the lady of the house, "you give us generously of your time."

"My visit is most necessary, ma'am, and I am at your service."

"You are solicitous of my welfare, sir, and I am grateful. But what further intelligence do you have so soon after your recent call?"

Adkins swept up the tails of his jacket and sat on a chair beside a small table. "My visit is in the nature of a further warning, ma'am. A house not far away has been broken open, which would indicate some criminal interest in the neighbourhood. But more, it is the home of an Admiralty man, and as your own home has obvious connections with the naval service the fact increases my suspicions. In short, there would seem to be someone inordinately interested in those who serve Britain on the seas. Or, at least, in their homes."

"Lor', you don't say so, Mr. Adkins."

"I do not wish to alarm you, my lady. Nevertheless, I thought it my duty to warn you further, especially as I was in the neighbourhood. Now I wonder if you could tell me —does my Lord Nelson keep any of his papers in this house?"

"I do not know of any. Why do you ask?' '

"Because he who broke open the other house might appear to have been interested in the gentleman's papers, and they were to do with His Majesty's ships of the line. I must confess I am quite baffled about the whole business, but I would hope to learn more in time. Meanwhile, I ask you further to take great care that your house is well locked."

"I promise to do as you say, Mr. Adkins, and to inform you at once of any suspicious event."

"Thank you, ma'am." The Runner possessed a smile that lit his face like a bright flame, and he bestowed it now

79

upon the shy Miss Hart. "I trust you continue to enjoy your stay," he said.

"I find it most agreeable," she replied, and Adkins persuaded himself that there was something quite special in her own smile.

"You are exploring the countryside and our London Town to your satisfaction, Miss Hart?" he asked then.

It was Lady Hamilton who replied, and he took a keen interest in her words. "Unfortunately my lord is away. Had he been here there would have been such a coming and going of his young officers that my niece would have been quite spoiled for choice of an escort. As it is, she has to put up with her old aunt wherever she goes."

"If—if Miss Hart would accept—I should be glad to offer—I mean to say, if Miss Hart would accept my offer, I should be delighted to escort her to any function where otherwise——" He was blushing and stammering, and it was not at all like the forthright Harry Adkins to be short of words.

"You are most kind, sir," said Miss Hart.

"Indeed you are," said Lady Hamilton. "If you would care, Rosemary? I am sure you could not be safer than with an officer of the law."

"Mr. Adkins, I should like it very much."

"Then if you are remaining here for some time, I shall be delighted." It was quite surprising how quickly he recovered himself. "At the moment I am much tied up by a number of crimes having occurred, but if I may present myself when I am less busy——?"

He took his leave congratulating himself on the success of his visit and a little surprised at the acceptance of his offer. But he need not have been. Already one or two of the cleverer police investigators were in demand by members of London society for whom they had solved crimes. From this it was to be a single step to a day only nine years hence when a Bow Street Runner named Townsend was to become a pet of the royal court.

So Adkins went back to London whistling a tune to the sunshine and the blue, unclouded sky—until he remembered suddenly that if there were some plot to break open Merton Place he knew nothing of it and was quite powerless to prevent it. And if it happened now, under his eyes as it were, what would Miss Rosemary Hart think of him . . .?

CHAPTER NINE

STEALTHILY, bearing no flickering candle, Jedd Stickles stole along the corridor of the servants' quarters at Merton Place and paused outside a bedroom in the darkness. Then, decisively, he gripped the handle, but the door did not yield.

"Who is it?" The words, in a feminine voice, came softly from within.

"It's me—Jedd," he whispered at the panels. "Quick—let me in!"

The door opened, and although there was no word of invitation, he thrust his way in. Before him stood a woman. All that could be seen by a single candle at the bedside, was that she had dark hair that had been unfastened and fell about her shoulders, that she was slim and that her eyes gleamed in the dimness.

But Jedd needed no bright lights to know many things about her, that she was young, pretty, white-skinned and firm-fleshed, that she had been an easy conquest to him (and to others before him, he fancied), and that she was as free of her charms as any lass in England. He felt that of this he was as good a judge as any, for was he not, by the same reckoning, the most triumphant wencher in England?

Their relationship was such that he now clutched at her with no preliminary courtesies. Wrapping her in his arms, he pressed his lips almost viciously on her cheek, her neck, her shoulder, stopping short of her breast, for it was covered by her bodice. Then he drew her to the iron bedstead in the little room and sat down on it. He held her hand, but she pretended hesitancy and did not at once join him on the bed.

"Down you come, Jenny, my love," he said, breathing hard. "Down you come, you gorgeous little bitch."

She sank down.

Unfastening the laces of her bodice, he said: "If ever you've envied Lady Hamilton, you can't have this long time, me darlin'! Poor dear, she's fine an' love-starved with th'admiral away. You, my pretty, you can have me most any time, eh? *I* don't go gallivantin' on the high seas."

"No, but you ain't no Lord Nelson!"

"What do you mean? I'm a sight bigger and stronger— h'and more handsome."

As she opened her lips to reply he smothered them with a long, bruising kiss, but she said as if there had been no pause: "That's as may be, Jedd Stickles, but you ain't got his money to buy me things with. I might as well sell my body instead o' givin' it free to the likes o' you."

"Shut up, you little whore. I'm doin' you a favour."

"I'm a-doing *you* a favour."

"All right, my pretty, I don't care who's doin' who a favour—so long as you get this thing off," he said, thickly, tugging at her bodice. "You should have bin in your night-gown by now—it's easier to get off."

He was relentless in his amorous fumblings, but talked glibly the while, his words trivial but his voice tense. "Your mistress is all right. Should be happy today, she should. Got a letter from *him* today, she did."

"How do you know?"

"Wore a flower in her hair."

"Ah, noticed that did you?"

"Ain't much I don't notice, me Jenny-o. What did his lordship tell her in the letter, eh?"

"Jedd Stickles! She read the letter to me, but 'twas private like. Private atween her ladyship and me. You just stop your pryin', Jedd Stickles——"

Abruptly conversation ceased. Garments strewed the floor. At last there was silence . . . a silence in which Jenny slept in Jedd's arms.

When she awakened he said, very softly: "What *did* the admiral write?"

"He wrote that he loved her," she murmured dreamily.

"What else?" He caressed her forehead with a slow, tired hand.

"He says as 'ow the French admiral—I think the name was Veelnerve or summat like—had gone from Toulon, but my lord Nelson gets it from a British commodore in the Portuguese service . . . wot was 'is name? . . . Oh, yes, Commodore Campbell . . . that the French admiral was amakin' for the West Indies . . . He wrote as 'ow it was not the first time this Campbell had smuggled intelligence to 'im w'ich 'ad proved to be correct . . . So 'e was sailing after him, he said . . ."

The voice of Lady Hamilton's maid trailed off, and she sighed contentedly.

Lazily he traced the contours of her face with his forefinger to keep her awake. "Did he put in the letter—anything about coming home?"

Her eyes blinked open. "He said—oh, yes, he said if he could find and engage the enemy then he might be able to come home to see her."

"Ah!" The exclamation was like a long and soaring note of music.

His eyes gleamed and his voice rose on a note of satisfaction. For those last few words, uttered so sleepily and with so little interest, they could surely put into his pocket yet another shining crown-piece.

"Ah!" he repeated, slowly, and fell into a doze.

It was as though Merton Place was a veritable breeding ground for sexual affairs of one sort or another. In its peaceful seclusion Lady Hamilton was not for the first time the mistress of a gentleman of importance; her grave-faced, demure-looking little maid was giving herself freely to the lustful Stickles; another footman was making clandestine and not unsuccessful visits to the housekeeper's room; and of a warm summer's night the pantry maid might be seen stealing quietly into the stable, where a groom waited for her in a nest of straw.

And now it seemed that yet another had fallen under the strange, amorous spell of the place. For the worthy Harry Adkins, usually all too absorbed in his work to take a second look at a beautiful woman, was determined to win the heart of one who was but a guest in the house. Be it said for his sincerity, however, that as yet he saw himself as a suitor rather than a lover.

So he came thoughtfully to Merton, wishing he could have seen her face when she read the letter he had sent paying his respects to her in the most polite and suitable terms, and stating that, if she pleased, he would find time on the following afternoon to escort her on a ride in the country.

What he did see, when he presented himself, was the smile she gave him and the light in her eyes that was as kind as candles' glow.

"You do me a kindness, Mr. Adkins."

"I do myself a kindness, Miss Hart, for I shall enjoy your company."

They took the lanes towards Wimbledon and rode out across the common. The miles of gorse, tree and bush stretched before them in the sunlight, and the wind blew fresh in their faces. An easy ride such as this, with his horse plodding and his senses tuned to the sights and sounds of the countryside was one of his favourite relaxations. But he was not relaxing now . . .

To him in particular this wistful, young woman had an appeal that was quite intangible, and though they rode in a tongue-tied silence her presence gave him no peace. To some she might have seemed quite plain, but at every turn of the track they exchanged smiles, and at these moments her face was transformed. They rode side by side, their stirrups so close that a bird might not have flown between, and he stole overt glances at her and was stirred beyond his knowledge.

"You do me a great honour, Miss Hart," he said at last, not realizing that the same words had been said before. "I find your company most charming."

"Nay, Mr. Adkins. It is you who are kind giving me a diversion from Merton."

"Do you not enjoy yourself there?" He was frowning suddenly. "I am most concerned."

"I find it most agreeable. Do not fear, Mr. Adkins. My aunt is very kind, and most solicitous of my welfare. It is only that she talks all day long of my Lord Nelson, and when she receives a letter from him there is no controlling her excitement, for she is like a country maid at a fair. I find it sometimes—just a little tiring, for it is not I who am in love with Lord Nelson."

"I am glad of it." The words escaped from him like a spoken thought, and he had scarcely been conscious of uttering them.

Her smile had gone and her puzzled face was upturned suddenly, but she did not speak. Tenderly, as lightly as a falling leaf, he rested his hand fleetingly on her arm. "I am glad of it," he repeated, this time with greater boldness, "for your love should be reserved for a younger man."

Her eyes danced mischievously. "Be he not so famous?" she asked.

"Be he never so famous."

They laughed together in some half-understanding, and the sound of it was silver like the beech trunks and golden like the gorse, for it drew their minds closer. It was one of those rare moments when time faltered before ticking on, and they both knew, suddenly and intuitively, that it had marked a step forward into friendship that would never be retraced.

"My aunt is always talking of young men, too." Her reserve had gone now, and with it her dignified politeness, so that she was for the time being her northern country self instead of the woman acting out a grander part. "She is for ever trying to find a young man for me."

"So I gathered when I called upon her."

"She is for ever thinking and talking of my Lord Nelson, so that one may think no woman ever loved a man more

86

deeply and more true. When he is at home she is at pains to feed and swell the remarkable esteem in which he holds himself, and when he is away she is for rushing about waving the letters he pens to her."

"My Lord Nelson is a most fortunate gentleman," said Adkins, smiling broadly.

"I should say he is, though sometimes I cannot help feeling a little sorry for his real wife, whom my aunt, for all her sincerity, has utterly usurped. Do you know there is something about Lady Hamilton's air that would seem to engender the most amorous feelings all around her?"

Adkins was serious for a moment. "Well, for one thing, if you will pardon my saying so about your aunt, all London knows the exact relationship between her and the admiral."

"I confess it must be so. As does her addiction to the bottle, with which she consoles herself to some tune. Indeed, I think her constant talk of my lord and the knowledge of her association has had some definite effect on her household. I see from time to time the most amorous glances between the men and women servants."

"I had not wished to talk of my work, but as you know I had thought your aunt's household in some danger. Now I wonder if what you say might in some odd way be connected with such danger?" The detective filed the thought in his mind.

"Why do you say that, Mr. Adkins?"

"Oh, only that a man in my profession leaves no stone unturned. But pray let us talk of other things, for am I not taking a diversion from my work? Allow me to say, Miss Hart, that however Lady Hamilton bears herself, I am most indebted to her for being concerned that you lacked a male escort."

"Oh."

"Yes, for I hope she has now found one for you in me— and that others may not take my place. Might I hope for such a situation?"

"Mr. Adkins, sir, you are most forward."

87

"Where you are concerned, Miss Hart, I intend to be."

The lady's cheeks grew pink in the cool breezes. "Perhaps I might be allowed to say only that I do not think the company of any other would be more agreeable."

They did not speak further on the matter, but looked at each other and smiled, for it seemed this was a better way than words of understanding each other.

They rode on in silence, deriving a contentment from each other's presence, until they had traversed the common and come out on to the Portsmouth Road near Putney.

Rosemary Hart reined in her horse suddenly as they came to the crest of a hill. Her eyes were fixed on the gaunt and blackened wood of an old gibbet, and her face was very pale. "What is *that*?" she demanded, pointing a trembling finger.

"It is a gibbet," he explained. "This road is notorious for both highwaymen and smugglers, and the thing was placed there many years ago as a warning to men who do not live by the law."

There was a wind on the hill, and the chains of the gallows creaked eerily. "Come, let us go," he said, gently, leaning forward and gripping the bridle of her horse. " 'Tis not a pleasant sight."

As they moved forward again her face was still drained of colour, and he was thankful that no human fruit dangled its bones from the high cross-piece.

"Oh dear," she said. "We were so enjoying ourselves. It has put me quite out of sorts."

"I fear it has, but you will have forgotten it in a moment."

As they cantered down the hill the incident put Adkins in mind of highwaymen and the new measures being taken at Bow Street to put them down. Perhaps Mr. Day and his patrol would in the end make it possible to remove such macabre constructions from the roads of England.

"I will show you something that should interest you," he said. "Do you see that building to the right, half-hidden in the trees? You are staying, are you not, in a house with strong naval associations? Well, that is an inn used as a place to pass on signals from the south to the Admiralty building in London. Come, we will take a look at it."

When they reached the building, Adkins pointed to the sign, which proclaimed its name as the *Telegraph Inn*. "See how aptly the place is named," he remarked.

They tethered their horses and sat on a seat beneath the swinging sign. The day was still warm, though the evening shadows would soon fall, and the two realized that they had made thirsty work of it with their long ride.

The detective opened his mouth to suggest he brought two drinks from within. But he did not speak.

A tall, burly man wearing a frogged riding coat and soiled cravat was coming out of the inn door. He paused in the shadows of the porch, looking keenly about him. Then he strode quickly to a horse, mounted it and was away, spurring rapidly into the distance and raising the dust as he went.

The sight raised urgent thoughts in the mind of the Bow Street Runner, who was on his feet in an instant, his mouth still agape and his eyes locked on the galloping figure of the horseman until it vanished among the trees.

For the man was he they called Gentleman Jerry, the fellow suspected of being a highwayman, the drink-sotted individual who had gone like a conspirator to meet the two strange fellows in Whitefriars—and what was he doing near to Wimbledon, where a house had been broken open, and in an inn where they dealt in Admiralty messages as well as dispensing ale?

CHAPTER TEN

For a moment the Bow Street Runner stared at the curve of the road round which the horseman had disappeared. Then he was striding for the inn door, quicker than one might have imagined for all his characteristic coolheadedness.

"Wait for me!" he said briskly to Miss Hart as he disappeared through the porch.

Inside, he accosted a man wearing an apron and clearing mugs from a table. "You, man, kindly tell me the name of the fellow who has just left."

"Er, wot man?"

"You know what man. The one who left this minute."

"Ah! *That* man. That 'ud be Mr. Bickershaw. Oh, aye, Mr. Bickershaw. That's the name, sir."

"Thought it was. Jerry Bickershaw, eh?"

"Aye."

"And what is his trade, eh?"

" 'Is trade?"

"His way of life, then."

"Don't know as I do know—and don't know as I should be tellin' if I did, sir, 'im bein' a customer and all." The man resumed his work.

The detective's cane cracked down on the table. "My name's Adkins. Adkins of Bow Street."

At the words the pot-man instantly set the mugs back on the table and gave his attention to the visitor. "Adkins," he said, drawing in his breath. " 'Arry Adkins. I've 'eard o' you, sir. Name's quite famous, for they say as 'ow you be the smartest Runner in town."

"As to that," returned the detective, smiling, "you must make up your own mind. But for the moment, my man, I should be glad of a ready answer to any question I might put to you."

The pot-man, who was very tall, towered over the detective, but nodded acquiescently. "Oh, aye, sir. Certainly, Mr. Adkins, sir."

"I should like to know," said the man from Bow Street, "what our mutual friend, Mr. Bickershaw, was doing in this inn?"

"Er—drinkin', sir."

"I am not surprised," rapped Adkins. "The fellow is much given to drinking. But what else?"

"Well, talkin'. Chattin', that is."

"With whom?"

"With one o' the Navy men."

"One of the Navy signallers stationed here?"

"Aye."

"In this room?"

"Aye."

"His name?"

"Well, er——"

"His name!"

"Abel—Abel Adams, sir."

"Where is Mr. Adams now?"

"Upstairs—in the room the Navy men use."

"Show me to him."

The pot-man hesitated. "Don't know as I should. I mean——"

"Show me to him this instant—in the name of the magistrate, Sir Richard Ford." The words were urgent, the voice calm.

"Follow me, sir." The man led to stairs at the rear of the building, and as he mounted them Adkins said: "Do not announce me, pray. I shall effect my own introductions."

"I'll but show you the door, sir, and make off," was the reply.

"Now why should you do that, eh?"

"I ain't 'aving nothing to do with it. That's why." With that the man jerked a thumb at a door and descended the stairs.

Adkins rapped on the panels, and as the door opened he found himself confronted by a big, muscular individual whose face was half-hidden in a huge black beard and moustache.

"Mr. Adams?"

"That's me."

"I should like a few words with you, Mr. Adams."

"Wot do you want?"

"If you will be so kind as to invite me inside, Mr. Adams, I shall be delighted to tell you."

The man remained silent, but he stepped aside and Adkins walked into the room, where a second individual, as tall and broad as his companion, sat on a bench at a table, breaking bread into a bowl of soup.

"Wot do you want?" repeated Adams.

"Well, I am more interested in the man you have been talking to, and who has just left the inn, than in yourself," said Adkins.

"Don't understand. Who be you talking of?"

"Come, Mr. Adams," persisted Adkins. "He who has just left. Mr. Bickershaw."

"Who *are* you?" parried the seaman, scowling.

"I am Harry Adkins, of Bow Street, London."

"Adkins the Runner?"

"The same."

"Ah."

"You are aware now of whom I speak?"

"Ah."

"Well, I am interested in what you spoke about when you met and drank together downstairs."

"Private," announced Adams, shifting from one foot to the other. "Private talk it was."

"Don't tell 'im anythink, Abel," cut in the man's companion, between mouthfuls of soup. " 'E's that snooper Adkins from Bow Street. We all know of '*im*. Don't never trust one o' 'is sort."

"I do not know your name, sir," said Adkins, evenly.

"But I must warn you not to impede an officer of the law in his duty. Kindly remain silent, for as yet I have addressed no remark to you. And as for you, Mr. Adams, surely you are aware that my business has much to do with conversations—even private ones."

Adams closed the door, very deliberately, locked it and slipped the key in a pocket. Then he advanced towards the detective, his face flushed, his arms bent and ape-like, as though he would grapple with the visitor.

Adkins heard the scrape of the bench as the other man stood up behind him.

Compared with the police officer, both the men were giants. Adams towered over him, his eyes glaring. But Adkins's stare was cool, unblinking, his face composed. He was not at this moment completely confident, but not a muscle betrayed the fact.

Slowly, almost delicately, he raised his amber-topped cane until the tip just touched the big man's chest. "If you please, Mr. Adams," he said. "In the name of the law, I propose to ask you some questions, and Lord save us, sir—I can hear your replies without breathing down my cravat."

Adams moved back a pace, as if the tip of the cane had been pointed steel.

"What did Mr. Bickershaw want of you?" demanded the detective.

"Nothin' special." A deep frown knitted Adams's brows.

"Well, what then?"

" 'E wus only friendly like. We 'ave 'ad a tankard together afore now."

"I see," said Adkins, not seeing at all. "You are employed by His Majesty's navy to transmit signals to and from Whitehall, are you not?"

"Correct."

"Was Mr. Bickershaw asking questions about any signals?"

"No, 'e wus not," lied Adams. "W'y should 'e?"

Adkins grinned darkly. "I do not know why Mr. Bicker-shaw should or should not. But there is someone not far from this spot who is interested in navy affairs. The home of an Admiralty official in Wimbledon has been broken open, and all his papers strewed about the floor."

"Well, they'll not get nothink from 'ere," growled Adams's companion. " 'Ouse is manned night and day."

"I hope not. Otherwise it will go ill with you because of what we know already. I shall take my leave. But I leave you with this warning—beware of anyone taking an undue interest in this house. Remember also, pray, that I have reason to believe that our Mr. Bickershaw may be—er, a suspicious character."

The cane rose again, this time pointing to the door. "You will need to use your key, Mr. Adams, before I can take my leave of you."

Adams unlocked the door and opened it. Adkins moved on to the landing, but turned before descending the stairs. "That will be all for now," he said. "But I may return to have further talks with you."

Escorting Miss Hart back to Merton Place, Adkins was at first silent and thoughtful. In the *Telegraph Inn* he had sensed something dark and sinister, and when that happened to Harry Adkins it was rarely due to imagination. The answers to his questions, he felt, had been far from frank. And Jerry Bickershaw? The detective was convinced that wherever the fellow went it could be on nothing but nefarious business.

CHAPTER ELEVEN

JERRY BICKERSHAW, the highwayman, was well content. In addition to his pickings on the road, he now had a regular source of income, for he seemed to be employed for a good deal of his time (when he was not drinking) by this man Bellamy.

What was more, the tasks he was given all appeared, so far, to be comparatively easy. For the man he met in White-friars he had passed money to one of the navy signallers at the *Telegraph Inn* in the hope, he presumed, of services to be rendered some time in the future. What use Bellamy might have for the seaman Bickershaw had no idea, and he was not the man to ask. In this particular matter he thought himself very clever in having handed over only half the payment, retaining the other part for himself as well as his own fee. What he did not know, however, was that the man from France, realizing this possibility, had given him a larger sum than might be necessary.

Next the highwayman's instructions had been to shadow Lady Hamilton's coach whenever it took a journey from Merton, but on no account was he to halt the carriage. Instead he was to make a list of the friends and relatives on whom the admiral's lady was in the habit of making regular visits. And while doing this he was to take note of the likeliest stretches of those journeys where a coach might be successfully attacked at some unspecified time in the future.

This was the business he was engaged on one moonlit evening when events took place that were to undermine his confidence . . .

The coach from Merton Place slowed almost to a stand-still to turn into the road from the gateway of the drive, and Miss Hart caught a glimpse of a dark, shadowy horse-

95

man standing very still on the grass verge. The figure lurked beside trees and hedge, and would have been invisible in the darkness had not the moon at that precise moment sailed free of cloud.

The coachman saw the dark outline, too, and with something of a shock, for horse and rider were not a foot from the roadway, and their presence startled the nearside animal in the shafts.

"Whoa there!" cooed the coachman, hauling on the reins. Then he upbraided the horseman. "Mind where you go," he shouted down. "You there—dost want to turn us over?"

Whereupon the observant Miss Hart saw the rider do a strange thing. He put an arm before his face, as though to hide it.

"Who was that?" she exclaimed, putting a hand on Lady Hamilton's arm.

"Oh, some fool no doubt," returned Lady Hamilton. "I should not worry, for our man has given him a piece of his mind."

But Miss Hart was not reassured. That was probably why she fancied she heard the sound of hoofbeats falling in behind before their coach gained speed and began to rattle and thud. She put her head out of the window and looked back. There was, she was almost certain, a shadow on the road behind. If the moon would but shine again . . .

"Rosemary, put your head in this instant," said Lady Hamilton. "You will catch your death."

"Aunt Emma, there is a horse following us," returned the young lady, excitedly. "I'm quite sure of it."

"Nonsense, my dear."

"Might I ask the coachman to stop?"

"If you must, my dear. But I am sure you are being much too jumpy."

Rosemary slid open a panel behind the coachman, who bent to listen. "Stop if you please," she ordered.

The coach squeaked and creaked to a halt, and as it did

so there were the unmistakable sounds of a horse in the rear. Then silence.

The coach moved forward again, and Bickershaw fell back to a discreeter distance.

Then the moon was silvering the roadway, and in its light the occupants of the coach saw another horseman riding towards them. But this was one they need not fear. In the pale light they saw him trim in his uniform, erect in the saddle, his hand easy on the reins. There was polished leather and a gleaming sabre-hilt, and as coach and rider drew near to each other he emitted a cheerful shout.

"Bow Street patrol!"

Bickershaw was too far away to hear the words of the greeting, though if he had he would not at that moment have appreciated their meaning. As it was, the highwayman thought the man a soldier, and he halted and watched from a distance as the coach drew to a stop.

The horseman rode up to the coach and saluted. "Bow Street patrol!" he rang out once more. "Is all well inside?"

"No, I am afraid it is not," replied Miss Hart, thrusting a white face out of the coach window. "We are being followed by a horseman, and we are much afraid."

"Drive on, ma'am, and have no fear," came the answer. "I'll settle his hash."

The patrolman's hand went smartly once more to his black leather hat, and he wheeled his horse's head in the direction from which the coach had come.

"Bow Street patrol!" he yelled, and this time it was no genial salute, for the words echoed in the night air like a battle cry for a cavalry charge.

And this time Jerry Bickershaw did hear the words, heard them ringing clearly in the moonlight and, for some reason he did not yet understand, very ominously. He did not wait to make the acquaintance of the uniformed man who was spurring towards him. Instead, he was wheeling suddenly and digging in his own heels.

As he fled he puzzled at the words that had rung out. The patrol was so new that he had not as yet heard of it. But there was no mistaking the name of Bow Street, and what it meant to a man who lived as he did.

Then there was no thought in his head but that of flight, and the wind in his face, and the cloud-free sky. Damn the moon and its clear, cold light!

He spurred and whipped, but the pounding of his horse's hooves was answered still and it was not his own echoes in the night. This man behind, damnation to him, too, for he could ride like a man possessed . . . The highwaymen of England did not know, as yet, what Mr. Day's old cavalrymen could do.

But Jerry Bickershaw, drunken sot though he was, could still give a good account of himself in the saddle. He left the road for the heath, putting his horse's head at a hedgerow and knowing what lay beyond, for this spreading common near Wimbledon was his own favourite haunt, and he knew every inch of it.

His moment of optimism was outlived, for over the hedge after him sailed Mr. Day's man, judging that where his quarry went he could go too. Bickershaw thudded on, twisting and turning and threading his way on the paths and rides he knew so well, doubling back, disappearing behind clumps of trees and hurtling out again to gain precious ground before the moon silhouetted horse and rider on another darkening ridge.

But the patrolman gave him a run for it. He chased him across the sleeping common to the Portsmouth Road, and beyond into Putney Heath.

Coming out of this heath, with the *Green Man Inn* solitary at a lane's end, Mr. Day's man found that his quarry had vanished with an astonishing suddenness.

At once the pursuer rode to the rear of the inn and accosted a stable-hand.

"Has a horse come in this minute?" he demanded.

"No, sir. Why do you ask?"

"Because I'm the night patrol, and I'm chasing a suspicious character. I ask in the name o' the Bow Street magistrates—has a man come in this minute?"

"There's bin not a soul this hour or more."

The horseman dismounted, ordering the stableman to hold the animal while he inspected the place. Moving from horse to horse, he found not one steaming and sweating in the stalls.

It was not the first time the stable-hand had hurried with Bickershaw's horse to a wooden shed in the orchard, and he smiled now in the shadows at the thought of the coin that would drop into his palm for his pains.

Later, from a secret, cupboard-like place above the inn's doorway, Bickershaw peeped through a small square hole in the woodwork and watched the man from Bow Street ride off into the night.

"I tell you, I do not like it," insisted Jerry Bickershaw. "They are setting against the gentlemen of the road a force with pistols and sabres, and they are men who know how to use them."

"Tut, man, it don't worry you, eh?" drawled the man from France.

"It does," maintained Gentleman Jerry. "It most certainly does."

"It don't worry me," said Bellamy.

"Of course not," the highwayman rapped back. "You don't take risks. I'm not acquainted with your business. I don't know what you're about, but you can sit there and smile, for you're in no danger. None at all, sir."

"I'm in greater danger than you can dream of." The frown on Bellamy's forehead was like a passing shadow, but his gaze was calm and cold.

"However, that's another tale, and we shall not pursue it. You make easy money from me, and you will not, in truth, allow the Bow Street office to stop you making it— just because they are playing at soldiers."

99

"*Playing* at soldiers?" Gentleman Jerry was incredulous. "The men of the patrol *are* soldiers. I'm telling you, one o' them chased me for miles. Like a leech on my tail he was, and he gave me a real turn. Rode me to within an inch o' my life. Made inquiries, I did. Used to be cavalry troopers, every man jack. They're soldiers all right."

"Yes—but *English* soldiers."

"I do not understand you, sir."

"Well, I have been a soldier myself, and I am sorry to say that I do not think the English soldier is the finest in the world."

Bickershaw, gazing at the man, could suddenly see the soldier in him, in his stiff-lipped hauteur and superior bearing. "Do believe I've rumbled you!" he said, his breath bated.

Bellamy took a small, neat pistol from his greatcoat pocket, idly examining its priming. "Speak up, sir, for you are most droll," he said, and Bickershaw did not like his smile.

"I've rumbled you," repeated the highwayman. "They've drummed you out o' the army, and it has soured you against the service."

Bellamy returned the pistol to his pocket. "Maybe you are right," he said, smiling more easily. "Who knows, eh?"

"You're a one, right enough," said Bickershaw. "You'll be saying next the English sailor ain't any good."

"On the contrary," came the reply. "I think the British sailor is a man to be reckoned with. And one in particular— why, I think he bids fair to be quite the most superlative. The best, indeed, that the world has ever known."

"Admiral Nelson."

"No less."

"Is that why you've got me hanging around his place?"

"It is. I should like to use him to my own benefit. Do not, pray, ask me what that is. Maybe I shall become a sailor, who knows? But to return to business. If you are afraid of this new patrol, you are of no use to me. Now speak up. I'm waiting, man."

"Well, I suppose I'll have to put up with the patrol."

"I suppose you will. You're not so puddled, I take it, as to be unable to keep your wits about you?"

"Damn the patrol," swore the highwayman, gently. "If one o' them comes too close, dare say I'll have to shoot him."

Bellamy eyed him closely. "There is a little matter I have wished to clear up with you," he said then, "and I think now as good a time as any."

"What is it?"

"Well, I do not know your life story, and I do not ask for it. But I fancy this country has not treated you quite a-right? You would not be in your present trade else?"

The highwayman clenched his fists. "It's right you are. Dead right. Born in a debtor's prison, I was. Killed my mother, it did. My father got himself and me out, don't ask me how. He built up his position again as a London merchant. Bought me a commission in the army. Then, hey presto, he was back in a debtor's prison again, and when I over-stayed my leave trying to get him out, I was cashiered for it. Drummed out in disgrace, damn them." He paused. "England?" He spat on the ground. "That to England!"

"Ah!" Bellamy's eyes were gleaming. "So now you are interested in but one commodity—money?"

"You could put it like that."

"Then you stick with me," said Bellamy, his lips twisting into an evil smile, "for the day may come when I might pay you a not inconsiderable sum for a service that would last no longer than it takes to pull the trigger of a pistol."

CHAPTER TWELVE

THE patrolman stood in the Bow Street Office reporting on his chase which had ended so abruptly at the *Green Man*.

"Can you describe the man?" asked Josiah Day.

"He was tall, easily six feet and more," supplied the trooper. "Very broad shoulders. Powerful, sir. Very powerful. Large, round face."

"Dress?"

"Greatcoat, civilian. Could be mistaken for an army coat, sir."

"Thank you," said the patrol conductor. "I do not suppose you saw his features, it being dark."

"It was night time, sir. But it was very light with the moon, and—yes, sir, there was something else. At one time I had nearly overtaken him, and he turned his face round. He had an old wound on one of his cheeks. I know a sabre cut when I see one, sir."

"Thank you," said Day. "You have done well. You may now dismiss until tonight's tour of duty."

When the patrolman had gone the conductor sat at his desk tickling the end of his chin meditatively with his quill. The description seemed to fit someone, but whoever it was he could not bring the man to mind. He shrugged his shoulders and began to write.

But suddenly he threw down the pen and rose abruptly to his feet. Why, yes, there *was* one who might fit such a description, and he was a man he had seen with his own eyes recovering from a drunken stupor in a den in Whitefriars—he whom they had followed to a tavern named the *Surrey Stingo*. Gentleman Jerry! That was the character. Gentleman Jerry who had met two others in that hovel of a tavern and bent with them like conspirators over a table in the shadows.

The patrol officer waited with impatience for any word of Harry Adkins, whose movements were as mysterious as those of any criminal.

In the afternoon the detective walked into the office, and in a moment Day had him by the arm.

"My friend," he said, urgently, "I have some intelligence from Wimbledon district that will surely interest you."

"Not about—Merton Place?"

"No, but about he they call Gentleman Jerry, he you pointed the finger to in Whitefriars and whom we watched together in the *Surrey Stingo*. Leastways, the description fits him, and he was chased by one of my patrols, not so far away from the *Telegraph* where you last saw him."

Quickly, the patrol officer recounted what had happened the previous night, and added: "I have put out the description to all my patrols and ordered each man to keep a lookout for him."

"Good man, Josiah," said Adkins. "There is something strange going on around Wimbledon Common, and Gentleman Jerry may be the key to it. I'd like him in for questioning." The thief-taker laid down his cane and gloves, perched himself on Day's desk and tilted his tall top hat to a more comfortable angle. "Now tell me, Josiah, this coach, where did it report to your man that it was being followed. Was it near Merton?"

"My man did not give the exact location."

"You will be aware, of course, why I ask. Jerry Bickershaw was to follow my Lady Hamilton's coach. Remember? I have already warned my lady of it———"

A clerk had approached the desk, and his voice interrupted the Runner. "Mr. Adkins, this letter was left here for you, sir. It was brought in by private messenger this forenoon."

The envelope was addressed in a neat feminine hand that was quite familiar to him, since he had now received several from the lady, and none had been concerned with business. He tore open the seal, and read these words:

103

To Harry Adkins, Esq.,
The Public Office,
Bow Street.

Merton Place,
Surrey,
Tuesday.

My dear Harry,

As you did ask my Aunt Emma some time ago to notify You Forthwith of any Strange Event in connexion with her House or her Coach, she hath given me permission to do so without loss of tyme.

It did happen late last night when my Aunt was called suddenly to a friend's sick bed—the verie thing you warned us of. Our Coach was followed by a right rascally ruffian, or at least I think he must have been such. He had lain in wayt for us at the gateway of Merton Place, and came on after we got on to the road.

My Aunt did not laye verie grate importance to the matter, but I could not do aught that would not be of benefit to your business interests, because as you know I think so highly of your dear self. So I notified a Bow Street Patrole, who rode off in pursuit of the scoundrel, and now notify your dear self.

I await our next meeting, which cannot come too soon.

Your friend ever,

Rosemary.

Adkins eased himself off the desk, smiling. "It *was* Lady Hamilton's coach, so I lay odds it *was* our friend Bickershaw," he said, brandishing the letter.

Day, who was as brisk as Adkins was lethargic, leapt to his feet so suddenly that his chair bowled over behind him. "I'm for Wimbledon without a moment's delay, Harry, where I shall join my patrols in person. I know the man's face, and if he is on the road I think we shall have him."

"Not so fast, Josiah, for I have a mind to ride with you," drawled the detective. "I may then pay a call on my informant, a Miss Hart, of whom I have already spoken."

"Of whom you are for ever speaking,'" smiled Day. "I'm for the stable to saddle my horse."

"I shall have *mine* saddled *for* me," said Adkins. " 'Tis just a suggestion, but if you can trust a groom to saddle yours also we could take a glass together while we're waiting, and I've a mind to buy you one in the *Brown Bear*. 'Tis right opposite this office, and we'll not delay."

"I fear I should not join you in a glass—I do not allow my troopers to drink on duty."

"An excellent rule—for the patrol," grinned Adkins. "But for the Runners, 'tis vastly different. For them more things are wrought by wine than this world dreams of. Without the talk in the taverns I'd never have taken a thief in my life."

"All right, Harry, I'll come across to the *Bear*. I'll have only one."

"Excellent, Josiah, but take your time over it, for I'm having *two*."

They entered the *Brown Bear*, a haunt of thief-takers and thieves alike, and emerged within the quarter hour, riding together for Surrey.

Adkins, who did most of his work on foot, set a slower pace than his friend might have desired, declaring that if they rode like the devil incarnate they would catch their man no sooner as they did not know where to look for him.

At the top of Putney Hill they parted company, the Runner jogging on for Merton, and the patrol conductor breaking at last into a canter along the Portsmouth Road to look for others dressed in blue—and a man whose face bore an old scar.

The evening had not yet cooled when Adkins reached Merton Place, and after the shortest discussion with Lady Hamilton he strolled with her niece in the garden.

As they walked down the formal paths, patterned by sops-in-wine and love-in-a-mist and heartsease, the still evening was full of the scent of lavender and gillyflower, and

Adkins placed an arm round his companion's shoulders. He did so with infinite care, lest he break the spell of their silent communion. They went as with a single will to a little wooden summer house half-hidden by climbing roses, and in its intimate shadows she came readily into his arms.

It was almost as though the amorous atmosphere of Merton Place stretched out even to this tiny retreat in its grounds. Almost, but not quite. For as it so happened the attraction the two held for each other would have been the same wherever they had met.

"I want you for my own," he said, using simple words for a plain, uncomplicated meaning, and there was nothing sudden about his statement. It was as though it were just a new movement of a symphony that had begun years ago on a garden path like this, and amid the trembling petals of its flowers . . . as though the words were expected to be said.

"It is what I want, too," she whispered, knowing now, as she had known for weeks, that she could give herself to this man and to no other, that she *would* give herself to this man . . .

In *her* case Merton Place *did* have something to do with it. She had met her man while staying with her aunt, and the aura of Lady Hamilton's love-life, pervading the house as it did, had brought Rosemary Hart to emotional maturity.

So their vows were made, as in an agony of breathlessness, as though no such eternal words had been uttered since the beginning of the world.

And there had never been an evening like it, as with their clothes rumpled and disarrayed, they made their way back up the garden path. They strayed off it on to the lawn, where flowers and shrubs made darker patches in the early dusk, and Rosemary caught her foot on a plant. His arm was already round her, and he had but to tighten his hold to support her.

"What happened?" he asked, looking down.

"I tripped over a flower or something," she said, bending

down and peering. "Yes, I see what it was—a clump of love lies bleeding."

Love lies bleeding! The words, at any time but this, were old and quaint and a trifle gay. Now, after their moment of passionate sacredness, on this fine warm night they fell upon their consciousness like drops of icy rain.

Love lies bleeding! He remembered that it was said by country folk that its red blooms were an imaginary flower supposed never to fade. What had been in the summer house heightened the perception of the usually unfanciful police officer, and it was no tingle of pleasure that made him silent now.

A shadow that was not of the night fell suddenly across his path.

For his part, Josiah Day was having a more active evening. "Stop every coach and rider, anything that moves on the roads," he told his men who patrolled this stretch of road. "Ask them if they have seen a man answering the description I have given you."

"Bow Street patrol!" The hail rang out at every mile, for on this summer's evening there were more than usual abroad.

"Gad, sir, what has the fellow done?" exclaimed the gentlemen who took the air in their phaetons and curricles.

"Is he a bad 'un, Mr. Redbreast," joked a coachman, staring down from his high seat at the patrolman's scarlet waistcoat.

Redbreast. The name was to stick.

But no one could recall having seen such an individual, not that day anyway. Two ladies being driven in a post-chaise swore that the man they sought was the very scoundrel who had relieved them of their jewellery a year come Michaelmas. But no, they had not seen him for many a day.

The exercise was not, however, without its value. It caused a deal of reassuring talk that at last something was being done to protect the innocent traveller on the roads outside London. The gossip was to spread, and the highwaymen themselves, of whom there were now so many, were soon to learn of the "Robin Redbreasts" who patrolled the highways they had thought their own.

Before it grew dark Day took his men off the main road. "I know that by my order the patrols are not supposed to leave the main highways," he told them. "But tonight is a little different."

They combed Wimbledon Common and the adjoining Putney Heath, stopping those on horseback and those on foot. Again they drew a blank.

At the *Telegraph Inn,* Day dismounted and threw the reins to one of his men. Inside, he spoke to the landlord, then stood on a chair in the parlour and addressed the company, most of whom were servants and country workers.

"Your attention, please," he called, and talk and laughter began to die. "My name is Day, of the Bow Street Horse Patrol, which has been founded to protect you all on the King's highway."

They gazed at the officer, impressed by his smart, double-breasted blue tunic, cloak and riding breeches. They saw the relieving white of his leather gauntlets, the polished yellow of his buttons, and they noted the businesslike sabre and truncheon at his belt.

"I should like you to help me, if you can," he continued. "I am looking for a big fellow with a scar on one cheek. His name is Bickershaw—Jerry Bickershaw, and I believe he can assist me in some inquiries I am making. Do any of you know the man?"

There was silence.

"Do any of you know *of* him?"

This time the silence was broken by a cough.

"If any of you should learn where I might find the fellow, will you kindly notify me?"

There was then a clearing of throats and a few grunts which the officer took to denote a reply in the affirmative.

At the doorway he paused. "I am to be found at the public office in Bow Street," he said.

A man sidled out after him into the darkness, and spoke behind the palm of his hand in low tones.

"You be wantin' Jerry Bickershaw?"

"That is what I said," declared Day.

"Wot will you give me if I tell?" Even in the dark a huge grin could be seen on the man's face.

"I'll give you a taste o' this if you don't," rapped Day, suddenly brandishing his truncheon with one hand and pushing the man by the throat against the wall of the inn. "Nothing if you do tell, but a crack over the head with this if you don't."

The man lifted an arm as if to protect his head. "I'll tell," he gasped. "I'll tell. But don't say it were me."

"I am not in the habit of harming those who help me," said Day. "Now quickly, where do I find him?"

"If you looks for a man, sir, then look first for a woman."

"Meaning?"

"That 'e is 'avin 'is way o' a servin' maid at the *Green Man*. Might be there now. Anyway, that's where to look for 'un."

"Her name?"

"Jessie—Jessie Jolikin."

"Thank you. If you are not joking with me, and if your information proves to be of the best, it may earn you a coin or two. But for the moment, get you gone and hold your tongue."

Day had two patrolmen with him, and mounting he ordered them to follow. In a few minutes they were at the *Green Man*, where the officer placed one man at the front door and another at the back. Then he strode inside, looked closely around and called for the landlord, who presented himself at once, his eyes wide at the sight of the unfamiliar uniform.

The patrol officer, his leather hat under his arm, introduced himself.

"I am at your service," simpered the landlord. "If there is any way I can help you——"

"There is," said Day, smiling. "I wish to see Mr. Bickershaw."

"Mr. Bickershaw? Can't say I know the name—not offhand like."

"Is there a man of that name here?" The smile was gone.

"Not to my knowledge. Bickershaw, eh? Don't know the name. But pray look around this room, sir."

"I have looked."

"Then I am afraid I cannot help you."

"I think you can. You have a servant by the name of Jessie Jolikin, do you not?"

"I have."

"Does she reside as well as work here?"

"Ye-es."

"Then show me to her room."

"I don't think——"

"Show me to her room—in the name of the law, sir."

The policeman was led in silence to the servants' quarters, which were situated, conveniently for a man like Bickershaw, immediately above the stables. The landlord pointed to a door, and a rapping on it produced a muffled gasp.

"Open up," shouted the innkeeper, finding the door locked. "A visitor for you."

There was a feminine shriek from within and an urgent scuffling sound.

Day flung his weight against the door and it crashed inwards. Flickering candles and the full, bright moon lit the scene in detail. Sitting on top of the bed, screaming lustily, was a completely naked woman, unable to make up her mind whether to use her hands to cover her breasts or her thighs.

Heaving at the window in an attempt to escape was the quite naked figure of Bickershaw. In one hand he held his breeches, hastily picked up from the floor at the bedside.

"I should not bother with the window, Mr. Bickershaw,"

said Day. "I have a man posted right below it, and you would but jump into his arms or on to his sabre."

The yells of the woman were now translated into a piercing caterwauling, for the innkeeper had given *his* attention to her, and was in the process of dragging her off the bed and belabouring her bare rump.

"Desist, sir!" roared Day. "I am not interested in the woman, nor in the sport she has just been up to. In the name of God, unhand her, for I cannot make myself heard in such bedlam."

The screams died to a wail, and the officer ordered the landlord to bring up the patrolman who was posted at the front door.

Day then placed himself in the bedroom doorway, twirling his truncheon and fixing his eyes on the suspected highwayman. He in his turn eyed his captor. For a single moment he thought he might try to rush the policeman, but there was a superior calm about the man, and a firm set to his jaw.

"Dress yourself," ordered Day.

Bickershaw dressed.

"What do you want of me?" he asked.

"I am taking you to Bow Street."

"What for? 'Tis no crime to tumble a wench."

"Agreed—and you are welcome to tumble her again when we have finished with you. We but think you can assist us."

"I can't."

"As to that, Mr. Bickershaw, we shall see."

They mounted him on the crupper behind one of the patrolmen, his wrists handcuffed, and the other two fell in watchfully at either side as they clopped down Putney Hill and headed inexorably for London.

CHAPTER THIRTEEN

THE Little Ferret screwed his face up into a grin that would have been positively wicked had it not been also impish, poked a finger playfully at his dashing new friend and observed with a wink: "Josiah, you're magnificent! Dragging a man from his love-bed, eh? I do believe the gentleman will never be quite the same again. The lovers' terror— that's you. You're a credit to the force already."

The detective then lounged back in his chair, rested his feet comfortably on his desk and added good-naturedly: "God be praised you were not at Merton Place last night. I was engaged in—er, somewhat similar sport. You might have had me up and about my business in no time."

"Never!" exclaimed Day, grinning broadly. " 'Tis only in the name o' the law I break open a love-nest. Never let it be said I'd do such a wicked thing to a friend. However, it's a good thing *one* of us was working."

"Really you're magnificent, friend," said Adkins, rising and slapping the conductor on the back. "Seriously, though, you've done excellent work. And now, let us have the gentleman in for questioning."

Their smiles had gone and they were both grave-faced when the surly Bickershaw was brought before them.

"I'll not stand for it," roared the highwayman.

"Then sit for it," returned the detective. "Take a seat by all means. We're quite polite here, you know."

"What do you charge me with?" demanded Bickershaw.

"Well, not for bedding a wench," said Adkins, flashing a smile. Then, stabbing a finger, he rapped: "What is your interest in Lady Hamilton?"

"Don't know what you mean."

"Why do you follow her coach?"

"I deny it."

"Why do you follow her coach?"

"I do not."

"We know you do."

"Prove it, then."

"That," said Adkins, "is what I intend to do—this minute. Mr. Day, could we please have Patrol Robinson?"

"Bring in Patrol Robinson." The conductor passed the order to a constable of the foot patrol, who stood at the door.

"Patrol Robinson," asked Day of the man who then entered the room, "is this the man you chased across Wimbledon Common?"

"It is, sir."

"I will ask my question yet again, Mr. Bickershaw," said Adkins, in a quiet, patient voice. "Why do you follow Lady Hamilton's coach?"

The highwayman studied his boots, as though he would find inspiration in them.

"If need be," said the detective, "I have all day to wait. Why do you follow Lady Hamilton's coach?"

"There is naught wrong in riding behind a coach," was the sullen reply. "I did not fancy overtaking it."

"If you did no wrong riding up behind it, *then why* did you make off when the patrol approached you?"

"Oh, ho, Mr. Adkins, no fool me. I don't want to get mixed up with your new-fangled patrol."

The Runner snapped a finger and thumb in the highwayman's face. "I am not surprised, sir, for I doubt it is not at all in *your* interest to do so." He swung round to Mr. Day's man. "Patrol Robinson," he asked, "are you prepared to swear before a magistrate that this was the man?"

"I am, sir."

"Hey, wait a minute," Bickershaw broke in. "You can't charge me with stealing aught. I didn't molest that coach——"

"So you admit following it?"

" 'Tis true I was riding behind it. But I did not molest it. Never molested a coach in my life——"

113

"Really, Mr. Bickershaw, you surprise me." The words were delivered in a studied drawl and with infinite sarcasm.

The highwayman was now obviously ill at ease. "Unless a man takes money or valuables you cannot bring him before a magistrate," he announced.

"For a man who professes such innocence, Mr. Bickershaw, you show a surprising knowledge of the law," said Adkins. "Now, sir, we shall talk of something else, if you please. The two men who set you prying on Lady Hamilton, *what is their interest in the matter?*"

The highwayman paled. "I don't know what—what you're talking of."

"Come, Mr. Bickershaw. You have an exceeding short memory. Mr. Day, is this not the gentleman we both saw talking to two extremely suspicious looking characters about my Lady Hamilton's coach?"

"That is so."

"Take the prisoner away," said the thief-taker, "and guard him well."

"You can't do aught to me," shouted the highwayman, as he was escorted out by the patrolmen. "I'm innocent and I swear it."

When he had gone, Adkins looked at Day triumphantly. "We can gain nothing by keeping the man in custody, but we can learn much by letting him go," he said. "Give me half an hour to effect a disguise. Then have him brought in and inform him he is free to go. I shall be lurking outside, waiting to follow him. I wager he will lead me to much knowledge."

As the thief-taker leaned against a sidewalk stump in Bow Street, waiting for the highwayman to leave, his own mother would not have recognized him. Gone was the tailed, top-hatted elegance; in its place was an aged jacket, patched and darned, and a soiled red neckerchief. The polished cane had been exchanged for a gnarled old wooden cudgel. And with the skill of a theatre make-up expert, he had made

114

his even features decidedly uneven; for he now had a crooked nose and angry bump on one cheek-bone that appeared to be the result of a blow in some recent scuffle.

The highwayman came out of the police office, walked straight across the road, looked both ways as of habit and disappeared inside the *Brown Bear*.

Harry Adkins sidled in to find him gulping a stiff gin to regain his nerve, after which the suspect hurried from the tavern and walked swiftly through streets and alleys. Several times he turned round, as if to check on whether he was being followed, but the thief-taker was a practised hand at shadowing suspicious characters, and the criminal did not catch so much as a glimpse of him.

Bickershaw made for a small court off Ludgate Hill, where he rapped impatiently on a door. His knocking was answered by a tall, slim, well-dressed fellow whom he addressed as "young Swift".

There ensued at the open door a hurried conversation, which Adkins, hiding in the shadows of a nearby alleyway, strained his ears to hear. He heard the word "justice" and "Bow Street bastards," and fancied that the man who went by the name of Swift spoke English with a very slight foreign accent.

"A moment, my friend," said Swift, disappearing inside and returning with a hat and cloak. The two then set off together, and Adkins, following at a distance, was not surprised to find them making their way towards Whitefriars.

As they walked on it was obvious that Bickershaw was telling of his lost sexual adventure at the hands of "a whore's son by the name o' Day".

"Oh, no, but it is unbelievable." Swift halted, giggling and pointing, and Bickershaw, unable to see the joke, glowered as though he would shake the laughter out of the fellow. "In matters of the female sex I am myself an expert, and I would not like it to have happened to me. And the poor little woman, she would not like it, either. I'll wager she won't have *you* in her bed again."

"But we laugh too much. It is serious what you say about Bow Street, but do not worry, for I will take you to them in a moment."

Soon the two had disappeared into a tavern, not the *Surrey Stingo*, nor yet old Fag's establishment, but an equally disreputable haunt, full of filth and distasteful odours. Adkins waited a moment, then sidled into the low-ceilinged, ill lit bar parlour. Peering through the mist of tobacco smoke, the detective allowed himself a half smile. It was as he had thought. In a corner sat the two individuals with whom Bickershaw had conferred before.

The newcomers were joining them, and the thief-taker glided noiselessly to a table not four yards distant, grabbing an empty pot from another as he did so. By the time the others glanced round, he was slouching as though half asleep in a chair, and with the appearance of having been there for some considerable time.

Adkins heard Bickershaw recount all that had happened since the patrol leader burst in on his privacy at the *Green Man*. Then the voices at the table were lowered and Adkins had to strain his ears. What he heard was this:

"I tell you, it's no good. They're on to me. They're on to you, too. So beware."

"Ridiculous. They don't know we exist."

"Oh, don't they? 'Saw you getting your orders', they said. 'Saw you talking to those two gentlemen,' they said."

"We're not so worried. Even if they've seen us, they don't know what we're about, for we haven't told a soul."

"Well, you'd better tell me what you're at, or I'll not do another stroke for you."

"Thought you liked the money we pay you."

"I do, but I'm beginning to think holding coaches may be less dangerous."

"I don't think so. *We're* not even asking you to rob, and that's all you can get done for. But there's another thing, Mr. Bickershaw——"

"Hush! No names, damn you!" The highwayman looked

round, gazed hard at Adkins for a moment, then turned uneasily back to the conspirators.

"All right. Now listen. We understand you do not—er, love England with a deep passion?"

"You know I don't. England never gave me a chance. We've discussed it, and you know it."

"Well, we don't love England, either. We'd like to—er, see some of her laws changed. And all we want is some information that would help us to that end. Now there's nothing wrong in that, is there? Even if you got caught. On the other hand, you get pinched for highway robbery and it's a rope round your neck—aye, until you are dead."

"I see what you mean . . ."

The voices dropped to a whisper, and not another word drifted to Adkins's ears. Bickershaw was a fool, he decided. There *had* to be more to it than a party of intellectuals in league with some scheming Member of Parliament.

The party rose and left the tavern. Adkins did not follow, for as they had whispered together each one had from time to time shot a glance at him. To shadow them now might ruin whatever knowledge he had gained.

But what had he gained? He called for a drink and sat quietly asking himself the question.

For one thing, he had an address near Ludgate Hill that at some time in the future might prove useful.

What else had he? Justice! By all the saints in paradise —Justice! The name clicked suddenly into place in the jig-saw of his thoughts.

From that alleyway near Ludgate Hill the word "justice" had floated to his ears as Bickershaw talked to the man called Swift. Then Adkins had thought of the word as a noun connected with Bow Street magistrates instead of a name.

But no, it was the name of a man—one of those who had just risen from that table, one of the two he had seen before with the highwayman—the one whose face he had sworn to remember.

117

And now he had indeed recalled it. Justice. That was his name. And what had the man done in the past to bring him to the detective's notice? Why, yes, he had once been suspected of assisting French prisoners-of-war to escape back across the Channel.

Adkins rose from the table, scraping his chair, spilling ale. Outside, he began to pace purposefully towards Bow Street, his eyes gleaming and a triumphant smile on his lips.

Justice was a spy. They were all French spies. Of course it was information they wanted. But not for England. For France. Admiralty secrets for France. That was it. The experienced thief-taker had been so right when he had sensed that something very important and dangerous was afoot not ten miles from the heart of London. Now he knew.

His inquiries had taken a dramatic step forward. But he was quite unaware, as he threaded his way through the unsavoury labyrinth of Whitefriars, that there was something else that the men from France desired—and that it was more vital by far than a handful of military secrets.

CHAPTER FOURTEEN

NAPOLEON BONAPARTE waited only for the situation at sea to change in his favour. Two splendid occasions had bolstered his massive ego, and the memory of their pageantry still lived. One was his birthday review of his invasion army at his camp overlooking the Channel. The other was his coronation in Nôtre-Dame.

But Napoleon I wanted to rule England as well as France, and up to now one thing prevented it—the British Navy. His plan had been for his own naval squadrons to escape from the ports in which the enemy had them trapped like rats, and win command of the Channel to free his flotillas at Boulogne for their assault on the English coast.

His Admiral Pierre Villeneuve was a fine sailor, but the emperor had long sensed that his sea commander was afraid of this poor, slim, sickly sea-dog named Horatio Nelson—and of his accepted genius.

Bonaparte had ordered his admirals to sneak round the British blockade, rendezvous in the West Indies and sweep back to a great sea victory. But Villeneuve's fear of Nelson was greater than his regard for Napoleon. The French admiral, having reached the West Indies, had been told to stay there for thirty-five days for others to join him. But on June 7, when he heard that Nelson was on his way to face the combined squadrons of France and Spain with only twelve ships of the line, he sailed for Europe to escape him.

It was indeed Horatio Nelson who stood in Napoleon's way.

Meanwhile, whenever a fast ship was sent with despatches, the British admiral was writing from his flagship *Victory* to his "dearest Emma" about what was happening on the high seas . . .

*I am chasing Villeneuve for all I am worth, but if I
fail to come up with him before I reach the Straits I shall
leave the command to Bickerton, and take their Lordship's permission to go to England to try to repair a very
shattered constitution.*

In such poor health was the man France feared. Yet he
was writing in these words:

*I had determined, notwithstanding Villeneuve's vast
superiority, to stop his career, and to put it out of his
power to do further mischief . . . I rather think he has
twenty sail-of-the-line . . . but we won't part without a
battle.*

These were the words that in a country house in an
English village were proudly read out by Lady Hamilton to
one of her maids. And they were words that, if they reached
the ears of *Capitaine le Vicomte de St. Remy,* alias John
Bellamy, would not be calculated to preserve the life of Vice-
Admiral Horatio Nelson, Duke of Brontë.

Innocent of this, however, Emma Hamilton read them.
But she did so also in the presence of Rosemary Hart, who
had taken a much more serious view than her aunt of some
recent and exciting news that Mr. Harry Adkins had been
at pains to impart to them.

As her aunt had unfolded the letter, Miss Hart had said:
"My dearest aunt, do you really have to read my Lord
Nelson's letters aloud?"

"Why ever not, child?" had been the reply.

"I but thought it unwise, that is all."

But the maid, hearing the short discourse, had taken note
of it. Consequently, when the letter had been read and Miss
Hart followed her to the door to close it, she at once put
her ear to the keyhole, and heard every word of the conversation which followed.

"My dear aunt, must you really?"

"Must I what, Rosemary?"

"Must you continue reading your letters to your maid?"

"Why not?"

"It is most dangerous. Aunt Emma, you cannot have forgotten the warning we have received."

"Tut, Rosemary, the girl is beyond suspicion."

"Nevertheless, the warning means we must trust nobody, does it not?"

"Oh, I suppose you are right. Very well, then, I shall not read any more of my dear Nelson's letters to her. But whatever am I to do? My dear man is so far away on the sea. Sometimes I feel I must pine away and die. If I cannot make an occasion of each precious word in his letters, how am I to exist?"

"Read them to *me*, then, Aunt Emma. I shall listen most attentively. Read them to me—but to no one else. You and I do not have military minds. How are we to know if there is that in the letters which might be useful to the King's enemies—to your own dear Nelson's enemies?"

"Very well, I shall read them to you."

"To me alone?"

"To you alone."

The maid tip-toed away from the door.

There was money in the admiral's letters, and the maid well knew it. For some time she and her lover had been sharing their good fortune as well as their caresses. She now moved from her position outside the door with a frown on her forehead and a pout upon her lips.

She found the footman entertaining the kitchen staff with bawdy stories and his own impression of an unlikely love scene between the famous admiral and his lady.

"Jedd Stickles," scolded Lady Hamilton's maid. "Do you ever think o' anything else but that caper? Come away this minute, for I've a message for you from 'er ladyship."

In the lobby outside she put her lips to his ear as he took hold of her. "When you come to me tonight," she whispered, "I've got summat important to tell."

"I know," he said. "A letter's come."

"Aye—that and more."

She struggled from his grasp at the sound of footsteps in the corridor and walked sedately off, re-arranging her hair and bonnet.

That night, in the intimate warmth of her bed, she told him what she had overheard. "Tonight is the last time, the very last time I'll be able to tattle about my lord's doings," she said, "an' this bein' so, I s'pose the money'll dry up?"

"Drat the woman!" exploded Stickles, sitting up in bed. "Drat the meddlin' bitch. Miss bloody-minded Hart, who in damnation does she think she is, eh? Why, she ain't h'even related to his lordship, for he and 'dearest Emma' ain't h'even married."

The maid sat up in bed, too, snuggling against his naked shoulder, but he thrust her away. "Put me right orf, it has," he muttered between clenched teeth. "Right bloody orf."

"S'pose there's nothin' can be done, Jedd?"

"Oh, isn't there?" he said, raking at his hair fiercely. "I'll bloody tell *him*, that's what I'll do."

"What can he, whoever he is, do about it?"

"Don't rightly know, but I'll bloody tell him. The bitch! Just when everything was going champion. Promised me more money than ever, he did, when the time came."

"W'en wot time came, Jedd?"

"'Ow the 'ell do I know?" In his exasperation the precise Stickles suddenly forgot to sound his aspirates. "Don't care a button for wot the gentleman's after, and 'e won't say neither. I'm entitled in my position to more money, ain't I? Take wot brass the good Lord offers, I says, and ask no questions."

In the house off Ludgate Hill John Bellamy held an extraordinary general meeting. He was never a man to smile much, but on this day his face glowered like an angry sky, and an atmosphere of foreboding pervaded the little room.

"I have called you together," he began, "to set our affairs in order, for some of them are not at all as I would have them. We must do better, gentlemen, than we do at this moment."

"What has gone awry is not the fault of any man in this room," observed Justice.

"Of that," said Bellamy, "I am well aware. But France will accept no excuse of me, *nor will I of you.* You all know now the nature of my mission. It cannot, must not fail. What I have to do I shall accomplish, and whoever gets in my way . . . God help him! If any man endanger my plan he will cease to live—just like that." The spy ring chief snapped his fingers. "If the most innocent hear a whisper of what is not good for them, they shall die before they can repeat that knowledge."

"Not a soul knows our secret," put in Justice. "I am sure of it."

"No, Mr. Justice, but there are now some who sniff at its edges. I refer to two gentlemen connected with the Bow Street Public Office—a Mr. Adkins and a Mr. Day. Already they have almost put Mr. Bickershaw, as far as we are concerned, out of business. It is with difficulty that we have persuaded him to continue in our interest. If these officers from Bow Street continue to upset my calculations they must look to their future—or lack of it.

"Furthermore, I understand a difficulty has arisen concerning our plans for making use of Admiralty signals to and from Portsmouth. Mr. Jamieson, this has been your special responsibility. Kindly report on it."

The man known as Jamieson took snuff and dabbed his nose with a lace handkerchief.

"A number of payments have been made to a person called Abel Adams, one of the navy signallers at the *Telegraph Inn* at Putney," he said. "Unfortunately, however, they were carried to him by this Bickershaw person, whom Adams learned was wanted by the law. He could not have failed to hear it, for this man Day, damn him, went into that very inn searching for the fellow. Now Adams wishes to wash his hands of the affair."

"The devil he does!" Bellamy did not move a muscle, but his eyes glinted dangerously. "Mr. Jamieson, you must use your initiative. Find something the man does not wish to be known, and threaten him with revealing it. All men have a secret. Discover his. It is imperative we have several sources of knowing my Lord Nelson's every movement and when he is to return to this country, and everything he may do when he has come home to Merton."

Bellamy then turned his eyes to one of the younger members of his team. "Mr. Swift, you have been set to ingratiate yourself with social friends of Lord Barham, His British Majesty's First Lord of the Admiralty. My Lord Barham is a gentleman nigh on eighty years, and perhaps a little foolish. Have you met him at any of the parties you have attended?"

Swift coughed behind his hand. "I have not, as yet, been introduced to him, sir, but I was at a party he attended, and have heard him discoursing at length, but only of the past when he was himself a sea captain.

"I have also been invited to parties at the homes of other Admiralty officials, but have not, as yet, gleaned anything that may be of use to you."

"Keep trying," Bellamy shot at him, "and *Merde* do not give yourself away. Now, gentlemen, it is my turn to report. I returned but an hour ago from a meeting with that bumptious footman from Merton, and I did not like what he had to tell."

"I never liked the fellow," said Justice, his smile sardonic. "I thought him a weak link."

Bellamy waved aside the interruption. " 'Tis not his fault. A weak link he may be, but his source of information was one of the best we had. I say *had*, for it bids fair to dry up."

"Mon dieu!" More than one breathed the oath.

"Lady Hamilton will no longer read out the admiral's letters to all and sundry," announced the spy chief. "Miss

Rosemary Hart, the lady's niece, at present residing at Merton Place, expressly forbids it."

It was as though the speaker had worn a mask which had slipped for a moment to one side. He rose, his face enraged, an evil light in his eyes, and for a time he paced the room. It was not the first time his confederates had seen him in such a way, and they waited in silence for him to control his feelings.

"Something must be done about Miss Hart," he said at last. "It must be something drastic, and it must be done without a moment's delay."

CHAPTER FIFTEEN

THE coach ground to a halt in the lonely country lane, and Jedd Stickles, wedged between Bellamy and Justice on the seat inside, had the sense of being a prisoner.

"What have we stopped for?" he asked, his face paling.

"For a talk," said Bellamy, confidently. "Just for a talk."

"What—what about, hey?"

"About Miss Rosemary Hart."

"Oh! Ah!" They were exclamations that simulated understanding, but the footman did not, so far, understand.

"I will explain," said Bellamy. "We are going to deny Miss Hart the privilege of remaining at Merton Place. We do not believe her to be a good influence on my Lady Hamilton. In short, Mr. Stickles, we are going to relieve the Lady Hamilton of the guardianship of her niece."

"You're going to—to abduct her?"

"If that is how you wish to put it—yes."

Stickles leaned forward as if to rise from his seat, and Justice placed a hand on his chest and pushed him back again.

"I—I will not be a party to—to such h'an outrage," stammered the footman, his face now the colour of his powdered wig.

Bellamy took from his pocket a small pistol and pretended to examine its priming. "All we want from you is some information. Does Miss Hart ever travel alone? What are her habits? That sort of thing——"

"I won't be a party to murder," cried Stickles. "I just won't. Not for any price."

"Who, my pretty fellow, said anything about murder?" Justice was smiling wickedly.

"You—you are not going to harm her?"

"We do not believe, as a general rule, in murdering women. Will that serve as an answer, eh?"

A little colour drained back into the footman's face, but he could not believe now what these men told him.

"I am growing a little impatient," declared Bellamy. "Think, man, of your own ends. If Miss Hart is taken away, who will Lady Hamilton have left then in whom to confide? Why, your own paramour. Which would bring the situation back to what it was—and put *you* back in business."

"You will not—murder her?"

"As my friend has said, we are not in the habit of murdering women."

Jedd Stickles did not believe them, and his voice quavered as he asked again what information they required of him.

"What are her movements?" rapped Bellamy.

"Well, I have never known her take a journey by herself, saving when she arrived at Merton."

"Is she ever alone anywhere, in Merton's grounds for instance?"

"Why, yes, every morning—if 'tis fine and sunny. My Lady Hamilton is a late riser. She drinks fair of the bottle at night. Waiting to breakfast with her h'aunt, Miss Hart takes a walk. She goes through the rose garden, on through part o' the grounds we call 'The Wilderness', out on to the drive and back to the house."

"What time?"

"Eight of the clock in the morning—if 'tis fine."

"What is this wilderness you speak of?"

" 'Tis a wild part, a thicket with trees and bushes and brambles."

Bellamy and Justice exchanged glances.

"Now listen, my man," said the former. "Not a word of this to a living soul—or we will ruin you. It would be a simple matter to write a letter to Lady Hamilton informing her, quite anonymously of course, about what you have been up to. Or yet one to Bow Street suggesting they send a Runner to talk to you about Miss Hart's unfortunate disappearance. Now is it a long walk from here to Merton Place?"

"Not—not far."

"Then I suggest you begin walking. I would not have us seen together just now."

Stickles tumbled out of the coach as though hell's hounds had been unleashed behind him. He ran, stumbling, for a few paces and turned to watch the coach trundling away. Then, turning his face to Merton, he began to wish wholeheartedly that he had never set eyes on these two rather strange gentlemen—or taken part in their business, which, whatever it might be, was stranger still.

Rosemary opened the casement on a July morning full of promise. An early mist lay in the hollows of the estate, but the air was already warm. She dressed hastily and came downstairs, passing many paintings and *objects d'art* and a beautiful marble bust of the famous admiral.

Jedd Stickles, who loitered in the hall, saw her descending the stairs, and thought her very pretty and dainty.

"Good morning, Miss Rosemary," he said, his voice lower than usual.

"And what a nice morning it is, Stickles," she observed, but the footman thought her smile a little too gay for a morning such as this . . .

Slowly, almost unwillingly he opened the door for her, and as she passed through into the porch she said: "Yes, a perfect morning, Stickles. Do you not think I shall have a most agreeable walk?"

"Miss Rosemary!" He took a step forward. "I should not——"

"Should not what, Stickles?"

"Should not——" He gripped the edge of the door. "Should not hope for a finer morning."

He closed the door gently after she had gone, and stood with his back against it, still holding the knob. Then he went into the cloakroom and sat down with his head in his hands.

Outside, Rosemary strolled through the rose garden, leaving the path and making marks in the dew. On she went to a walk which Lady Hamilton had had specially constructed so that Nelson might feel himself on his own quarter-deck.

It was this walk which led to the round, white summer house frequented of late by herself and Harry Adkins—and which had been christened The Poop.

She stood for a moment looking into it, sighing luxuriously, then walked on towards that part of the grounds they called The Wilderness.

The birds were chattering the morning to life, but as she entered the thicket they rose in raucous alarm, circling watchfully. They might have been birds of prey, she thought, rather oddly, were they not so small.

She walked on, and there were patches of shadow now where the sun did not come . . . Somehow the thicket was a little gloomier this morning, the worn path darker . . . But soon she would have left The Wilderness and reached the bright, wide drive . . .

At first she thought a tree branch had snapped and that she was being smothered by a mass of soft leaves. But at once she was conscious that it was a blanket that had been thrown over her head. She was gripped so firmly from both sides that her struggles were useless. She was hurried along and it was like a nightmare, for she could not see where she was going, and the blanket was muffling her screams.

At one point she stumbled and fell, and the blanket partly left her shoulders. She could not see her attackers, but she let out a piercing scream before it was drawn tight again.

The coach into which she was bundled had been rolling for some time before the blanket was removed from her head. She looked fearfully around her—to find herself imprisoned between two strong young men wearing black masks.

They were not of a ruffianly type, both being dressed in the mode, but their eyes were grave behind the slits of their masks, and it was no youthful prank.

"What is the meaning of this outrage?" she demanded, panting from her rough handling.

"It is quite useless to ask questions," said one, "for you will receive no answers."

"Where are you taking me?"

"Hold your tongue, for we have no great wish to speak," muttered the other.

The two men sat in silence then, morose and solemn, as if they had no liking for what they had to do.

There was little chance that they would tell her who they were, for they continued to wear their masks. In fact they were the young French spies who used the names of Swift and Speed, who had been warned long ago to expect that their work would not always be agreeable. And it was not agreeable now.

In the house they had left Jedd Stickles gradually recovered his nerve, but for the rest of the day was to move about like a man who waited for something unpleasant to occur.

In the grounds the head gardener, Thomas Cribb, attended to his chores. Earlier, he had thought he heard a single scream from the direction of The Wilderness. But whatever it was it was not repeated, and he had decided it was the alarm cry of a bird, echoing strangely from a distance.

CHAPTER SIXTEEN

THE messenger from Merton Place, hot and dishevelled from his hard ride, stumbled into Bow Street police office. "Mr. Adkins!" he cried. "I must see him at once."

The next minute, standing before the detective, he was exclaiming: "It's Miss Hart, sir—she's gorn, vanished, sir, and leaving no trace."

The one moment the cool Mr. Adkins was lounging at his desk. The next he was leaping to his feet so violently that his chair was crashing over.

On the instant he was a man transformed. Gone was his exasperating drawl; in its place came an incisive voice. For once the man of thought was one of action, and he was issuing orders so fast that they appeared to dove-tail into each other. "A chair for this man. Bring him refreshment. I'm off to Merton. Not my old nag. A light, fast carriage. Fastest you can get. Quickly. In the name o' God, hurry."

Then he was doing several things almost at once, jamming on his topper, reaching for his cane, snatching up his cloak. He paced the office, peered out of the window, rapped his cane on any object that was to hand.

At the right moment the deep-thinking, slow-moving, comfortable Mr. Adkins could move—and move quickly—but never before had they seen him quite like this.

They had secured for him a small, open chaise, hired sometimes for police business, and as it drew up outside Adkins leapt up beside the driver almost before it was at a standstill.

"Merton!" barked the dective. "Wimbledon way—and make this thing spin. Drive like the devil's at your back."

Impatiently the detective slapped the palm of his gloved hand with his cane as the two horses, high-stepping and nervous, set off towards Westminster, picking their way through the city traffic. Progress was little faster down The Strand, filled as it was with carriages from the mansions which stood off this road in gardens running down to the Thames.

But soon they were in the Old Brompton Road, posting through fields and trees and market gardens, and Adkins content with nothing less than a perilous pace.

"Get those animals moving," he exhorted the driver. "Crack that whip, man."

This chaise and pair, he knew of old, was as fast as any of the famous "Tally-ho coaches," which could average ten miles in an hour.

"Faster! Faster!" The wind whipped the words from his mouth as they rattled over Putney Bridge and the horses settled to the long pull up the hill.

" 'Ave 'er over, you will," shouted the driver, thankful for the moment that the hill was reducing the mad speed.

"Don't care what happens," bawled Adkins, "just so long as you get me to Merton at the soonest."

At last they were turning into the driveway of the country house and Adkins was leaping down almost before the carriage had ground to a halt. He left the driver still perched on his seat, mopping his brow with a huge, red-and-white, spotted handkerchief, and nodding in reply to an order for him to wait.

The detective belaboured the door with both his cane and the knocker.

It was the footman Stickles who opened the door, pale and apprehensive, aware at this startling moment of the identity of this dandified, eye-twinkling character who had appeared so pleasant and harmless when he had waited upon —upon, of all people, Miss Hart. But to the footman he was now like a stranger, for his brow was dark and his eyes glinted dangerously.

"Why, Mr. Adkins, sir——" he began, but the famous detective was striding into the hall, eclipsing the servant's words with those of his own. "Lady Hamilton. Tell her I am here. This instant."

When Stickles had taken the visitor to her ladyship he went to the cloakroom and sat heavily on a chair.

The Little Ferret! So this was the famous thief-taker. He had not hitherto connected the name of their affable visitor with that of the Bow Street Runner. Adkins. The name was common enough, and he had known him only as "Mr. Adkins."

But that morning he had heard that her ladyship had sent to Bow Street for Mr. *Harry* Adkins. And now Mr. Harry Adkins had arrived. God save the trembling footman, but what a foolish thing it had been to play tricks with the lady of—*The Little Ferret*.

In the drawing-room Adkins resumed the pacing he had begun in his office.

"You have no glimmering of thought, my lady, where she might be?"

"None."

"She said nothing that one might connect with her disappearance?"

"Not a word. Oh, Mr. Adkins, I do not know what to do."

"Please, my lady, try to calm yourself. Has any horse or coach gone from your stable?"

"Not a one, Mr. Adkins."

"You say she did not return from her morning walk," mused the detective. "Does she ever walk beyond the grounds?"

"I have never known her do so."

"Have you had the grounds searched?"

"Every inch of it. Cribb, the head gardener, has had all his men out, and every man from the house with them."

"Was she—herself—before she retired last night?"

"Quite her usual self."

A thought flashed. Had she walked far beyond the grounds and had an accident? Did she lie this minute injured and alone? He paused in his pacing and gripped the chair back.

133

Then he moved about the room again, eyeing ornaments and *objets d'art,* seeking inspiration, thinking deeply . . .

The detective's intuition had not played him false. From that first visit to the *Surrey Stingo* he had been convinced that he was on to *A Case.* It had seemed then that a robbery was being planned, in this house or on the highway. Gradually The Plot, as he had dubbed it, had widened and taken on some mysterious admiralty and naval significance. Then he believed that a spy ring was in operation. Finally, his own Rosemary had disappeared, and what in God's name could the connection be?

The Mystery of Merton Place was deepening . . .

Again he paused in his pacing, this time lowering himself heavily into a chair, for an astounding thought had entered his head. Could Rosemary be connected in some way with the spies? It was a dreadful, impossible thought. For a moment its impact stunned him.

He must find his Rosemary, and he must find her safe, for he would with his own hands squeeze the life out of any man who harmed her. He was driven to find her, yet what if his investigations pointed a finger at her?

Rising, he drove the idea from his mind. But as he did so he realized that falling in love was not all honey sweet, for it had now sent him down a dark path, and he did not know the end of it.

"I suggest you take a rest, my lady," he said, "and in the meantime I should be obliged if you would arrange for me to see every one of your servants. Please to have them sent in one by one."

The cook was so loquacious that in her ¡ resent excited condition she was of little help.

The kitchen maid was so terrified and tongue-tied that she was of no assistance at all.

Stickles was the last to have seen Miss Hart, but he had merely opened the door for her as she went out. No, there was nothing unusual in her manner. Happy and smiling she was.

134

"Could have knocked me down with a feather, you could," confided the footman, forcing a smile where there was no will to smile. "Disappeared into thin air she has."

Adkins, who had never liked the fellow, was more than ever convinced of the fact. But he was too experienced a thief-taker to forget the dangers of allowing personal feelings to influence his mind.

"It's certain sure she ain't here, Mr. Adkins," added the footman, "so where will you look?"

"Have you any ideas, then, where I might look?" asked Adkins, laconically.

"No, sir. None whatsoever."

"Then do not waste my time. Now please to send in the next person." Stickles turned to leave, but Adkins spoke again. "Oh, and Stickles—I may well have to talk to you again as you were the last to see Miss Hart."

My lady's personal maid had not that day seen "the missing person", as she put it. Seldom did till after breakfast. Adkins thought her manner a trifle saucy—and the neckline of her dress too low for a lady's maid.

None of the household servants could throw the merest glimmer of light on the affair, and the detective took snuff as he waited for the garden and stable staff to come before him.

One of these was an ageless individual with a pleasant face the texture of leather and the colour of old oak. "Me name's Cribb," he said, with a smile as slow as the changing seasons. "I be the 'ead gardener."

For the first time that day Adkins's face relaxed as he returned the smile. "You will know Miss Hart?" he asked.

"Ah do and all," said Cribb. "Lovely lady, 'er be. She loikes gardins—so I loikes 'er."

The thief-taker smiled again. "You were working in the garden when Miss Hart went for her morning walk?"

"I allus am."

"Did you see her?"

"Caught a glimpse of 'er once."

"Which way did she go?"

"Through rose gardin, along Quarter Deck to Poop, then through Wilderness. She allus does."

"Did you see anything extraordinary, anything *different* this morning?"

"Can't say as I did."

"Did you then—*hear* anything odd?"

"Hear aught? No, sir. Usual mornin' sounds. Birds singin' ... *Birds*——" He broke off and fell to scratching his head violently. "Danged if it ain't funny, sir, now you mention it. I 'eard a sound like a bird screamin'. It wern't like any bird I knows, but I thought mebbe it were a strange 'un givin' throat——"

"Where did the sound come from?"

"From t' Wilderness. From that way on."

Adkins was striding for the door. "Come, my good man. Show me where you thought it came from."

Servants crowding the hall watched in silent awe as the two hurried from the drawing-room and left the house together.

"Wot the 'ell's 'appening?" hissed Stickles, forgetting his aspirates in his alarm.

"Gawd!" breathed the dark-haired girl at his side. "Oh, Gawd!"

The two men made haste through the rose garden and past the summer house, but as they reached The Wilderness Adkins raised a hand. "Steady!" he ordered. "Slowly now if you please. If there is the smallest clue to be seen I do not intend to miss it. Now where would you think the noise came from?"

"From other end o' this track," said the gardener, pointing to a path beaten by feet through the thicket.

Adkins moved slowly, examining the path and its surroundings. He reached the end of it, halted, tilted his topper with the knob of his cane and puckered his lips thoughtfully. He had found nothing. Then he jammed down his hat again and began to retrace his steps, this time moving slower still.

136

"Wot be you a-lookin' fer?" asked Cribb, following closely.

"I do not know myself," muttered Adkins. "But pray do not talk or I shall find nothing."

They had gone perhaps a quarter of the way back down the path when Adkins halted abruptly. It was a spot where branches of tall evergreens roofed the track, keeping out the sunlight on the brightest day. The shadows clung like evil thoughts. This dark tunnel was a natural secret place that had in its time given shelter to lovers and their fumblings—and to desperate men and beings that scuttled from the light. Adkins was conscious of it as a place with many secrets to keep. He strained his eyes.

Suddenly the tip of his cane pointed, and Cribb saw that the long grass had been newly trampled behind a tall bush. The cane moved again to indicate a similar area of crushed undergrowth at the other side of the path.

"Just the spot where rogues would lurk, eh?" Adkins spoke meditatively, as though he did not require an answer.

"Ah," said Cribb, his voice hushed, aware that no more help was expected of him.

"Yes, this is the spot." The thief-taker was thinking aloud. "This is where it happened."

"Where wot 'appened?" breathed Cribb in awe.

"That we do not yet know," said the detective, suddenly brisk again. "Come."

He returned to the end of the thicket. Here the track led to the left towards the drive and the tall gates. Hardly the way a criminal would take, he decided, turning to the right instead, where there was soft earth and no path.

In a few moments he was staring down at three sets of newly-made footprints. One set of tiny heel and toe marks was flanked on either side by two others, and *they* had been made by heavy boots.

The prints led to a high hawthorn hedge that flanked the roadway—and to a narrow gap through which a man might squeeze. As he approached, something small and white arrested his eye, adhering to the thorny fronds where the hedge parted. He took it in his hand. It was a lady's handkerchief.

Pushing through the hedge, Adkins began to pace the grass verge to the roadway until he found something for which he now apparently searched. He was not long in finding it—wheel and hoof marks where a coach had waited off the roadway.

He turned without a word, and walked to the gates and up the drive towards the house.

His brow was not now quite so dark. He concluded that Rosemary had been taken away against her will. Thank God she was not, it might now seem, a party to any dark conspiracy. But the gleam of relief died as it came, for it diminished not one jot the peril in which she lay.

He quickened his pace on the gravel.

CHAPTER SEVENTEEN

This time he questioned only Lady Hamilton, for there was something he had to do and it was more urgent than talking.

"Please to examine this," he said, handing to her the handkerchief. "Do you recognize it?"

"I do—it is Rosemary's."

"It bears no mark—how do you know?"

"I gave it to her. It is as you see edged with fine lace. I know it is the one I gave to her. Where—where did you find it?"

"At the edge of the grounds."

"What—what does it mean?"

"I may hazard a guess, but I do not know for certain what happened." Adkins moved to the window and looked out on the garden, gay and peaceful in the sunshine. "Lady Hamilton, if there were they who wished to pry into the secrets of war—my Lord Nelson's secrets, for instance—would you expect them to discover any in this house?"

"I do not think so."

"Why not?"

"As far as I know he has no papers of consequence in this house. He has them all in the Victory, where his two secretaries have them in their keeping."

The detective moved from the window to the fireplace, where he remained silent for a moment, staring at the unlit logs. "Do you yourself know anything about Lord Nelson's plans?" he asked.

"Nothing of any importance," declared Lady Hamilton. "I am quite sure of that."

"I should be obliged if you would allow *me* to be the judge of that. Please to tell me, if you will be so kind, what you know of his present plans, if any?"

Lady Hamilton put her fingers to her brow, an action designed to induce thought. "Let me see. The French Admiral Villeneuve managed to slip out from the British blockade and scurried off to the West India islands. My dear Nelson chased there after him. Villeneuve must have been mortally afraid of my man, for though my lord had only fourteen of the line, the French admiral ran away from him, sailing towards Europe.

"Now what else do I know, Mr. Adkins? Why, yes, on the 20th of last month of July my dear lord was anchored at Gibraltar and went ashore for the first time in two years. He had been at sea the whole of that time engaged on what he called The Long Watch."

"Do you know where his lordship is now?"

"I would say he is under sail—for home. I understand there is little more he can do at sea—for the moment."

Adkins gave her a searching look. "My lady, I do not wish to pry, but I am afraid I must ask you—how did you come by this knowledge? Your answer may be important."

"Why, from the letters he sends to me whenever one of his frigates sails with despatches. How else?"

"Again I do not wish to pry, but does Rosemary know also what movements my lord makes at sea? Have you discussed these things with your niece?"

"This last while I have read out the letters to her. Do not blame me. They are all I have had these two long years—his letters."

"Who knows you have done so?"

"My friends."

"What friends?"

"My lord's brother William, for one. Mrs. Embleton, of Bath. My dear Mrs. Emery, of Kingston. Oh, and many more. Many of my friends."

"Do any of these friends have contact with any who may be connected with France, any person of French birth, for instance, any of those *emigrés* who have settled in England?"

"It is hard to think." Confused and excited, Lady

Hamilton was clasping and unclasping her hands. "Why do you ask so many questions, Mr. Adkins?"

"In the first place, it is my duty," said the detective, tersely. "In the second, I wish to find your niece—for my sake as well as yours, you will understand."

"Of course. I will try to think. Mrs. Embleton once told me that she suspected one of her friends was really a French lady who had been smuggled to England as a child during the Revolution. There may be others. If I think of them I shall tell you. What does all this mean? How will it help you to find Rosemary?"

Adkins was at the door, his fist on the handle. "I have not time to explain, even if it were wise. Nor is it wise for you to tell anyone what we have discussed—anyone at all, you understand? I shall return to ask you more about your friends. In the meantime, however, I have something urgent to do. My lady, trust me to do the best I can. I swear that I shall leave no stone unturned to find Rosemary—and pray God she is unharmed."

When he had gone Lady Hamilton wondered if she should have told him that Rosemary was not the only woman in the household to whom she had read her letters. Perhaps it was of little importance, for it was Rosemary who was missing and not her maid. If she remembered, she might tell him when next he came.

Posting to Bow Street, demanding of the driver more speed at every mile, Adkins was conscious of an omission on his own part. He should have advised her ladyship that in the future she should not read a word of her letters to any of her friends, or to any living soul. But perhaps this had not been necessary after all, for even Lady Hamilton, indiscreet as she was, must realize now that something very dangerous was afoot. Thinking of what must be done, and the plans he must make, he dismissed the thought from his mind.

Sir Richard Ford listened gravely to the information the detective laid.

"If your suspicions are proved correct, Mr. Adkins," he said, "then the position is of the most serious. The Admiralty, indeed the government must be informed at once, and I shall see to it. I have no doubt that as a result your services will be retained by the government, as they have been in similar matters before."

Then the magistrate allowed himself a fleeting smile as he added: "It would seem, Mr. Adkins, that this time it will be spies and not thieves you will be trying to take."

"Just so," agreed the detective, rising, "and in the meantime may I have your permission to continue my inquiries at once?"

"Certainly," said Sir Richard, "and I warrant that within the hour you will have Mr. Pitt's also."

"Thank you, and one thing more. It is most urgent. I believe I have discovered the house where the spies—if they be—are residing. It is a lodging in a court off Ludgate Hill."

"Excellent!" exclaimed the magistrate.

"What is more, I suspect it may be there that Miss Hart now lies. I do not know in what peril she finds herself, but with every minute the danger must increase. I ask your permission to raid that house—without a minute's delay."

"I think that in the circumstances I can take that responsibility. Raid the house if you think fit. Take whatever you require of Mr. Stafford's or Mr. Day's, whatever force you think necessary." The magistrate was reaching for his hat. "And while you are at it, I shall be on my way in person and this minute to Westminster with these alarming facts."

Leaving the magistrate, Harry Adkins at once invited Mr. Day and Mr. Stafford, chiefs of the horse and foot patrols respectively, to a small room used for interrogating prisoners. The detective locked the door before joining the two round a table.

"I do not wish to be disturbed," he explained, "for what I have to say is more important than any other business at this office. Neither do I wish to be overheard, even here, for it is to do with the welfare and safety of the country— or so I believe."

The conspiracy had become known to him and Day as The Surrey Plot, but the patrol officer was as yet unaware of the last two startling developments—that it appeared they who spied on Merton did so for France and that Miss Hart had vanished.

"In the name of God, gentlemen, I now seek your help," said the thief-taker when he had told all he knew.

"You can count on me," said Stafford.

"And on me," said Day.

"Excellent!" said Adkins. "Then how do you think we should go about it? In the matter of breaking into that house you are the experts—though I shall not be left behind when you do it."

"I would suggest," said Stafford, "that *my* men would be better for closing in on the house, for though armed they do not wear uniform and there would be less chance of raising an alarm."

"That is so," agreed Day, "but I think I should take some of mine, to hold in readiness with their mounts in some hidden places. If any should escape on horseback after you have entered the house they could then be pursued to good purpose."

They discussed their plans carefully. Mr. Stafford decided to take with him two captains, each with his four men, Mr. Day half a dozen horsemen.

Then the horse patrol conductor changed into a civilian suit and set out with the other two to reconnoitre the small court and its vicinity.

Day picked suitable alleyways near Ludgate Hill which would give shelter to his men some distance from the house. Unfortunately from none of these could the small, square court be surveyed, but he decided that he would himself be within sight of the house and a pistol shot would be a signal to his men if any attempted to escape.

Neither Adkins nor Day showed themselves in the court itself, for they might be recognized if Bickershaw entered or left the house.

Chief Inspector Stafford discovered a number of streets and lanes by which one captain and four men could position themselves at the rear of the house without the necessity of crossing the court.

This party left Bow Street first and went into hiding with the back door in view.

Next Conductor Day, mounted but in civilian clothes, deployed his men and waited in the court for the arrival of the others.

Then Adkins and Stafford set off with a second captain and four men. They made their way along Fleet Street and into Ludgate Hill. The sun was going down, but its rays were still strong enough to glint on the captain's carbine and brace of pistols and the hilts of his men's cutlasses. They marched purposefully, yet no head was turned among the evening strollers, for the foot patrol was now an established force in the city.

They entered to find the court deserted save for a gentleman in a shady corner of it dressed in a russet tailcoat and riding boots, and apparently having trouble with one of his horse's hooves. This he was examining as though searching for a stone. Adkins and Stafford were careful to ignore him.

The clatter of the patrolmen's boots on the cobbles echoed in the little square, and a man glanced down from a second-floor window. The squad halted not outside this particular window but beneath those of a house at the other side of the court. Yet the onlooker took a step backwards from the casement and stiffened. He was the man from France known as John Bellamy, and it was not *his* lodgings in which the patrol were interested but those opposite. The spy was much too clever to reside in the house at which his contacts were asked to call. That was the lodging of Speed and Swift.

Bellamy's eyes were rooted to the scene below. "Do not come too close to the window," he breathed, "but what make you of this?"

Justice and Jamieson, who were also in the room, moved nearer and peered down. They saw seven men and the gleam of steel. They noted that one, not so tall as the rest, was unarmed. He carried only a cane.

"It's the patrol," said Justice. "It would seem also to be serious. Why else would its Chief Inspector, Stafford, be in attendance?"

"You recognize this Stafford?"

"I do. I made it my business, long before you came, to know the likeness of the man."

Bellamy swung round. "Jamieson," he hissed, "saddle the horses this instant."

Jamieson left by the back door, which was not watched like that of the house opposite, and hurried down a lane to open the wooden door of a stable. He had plenty of time to complete his task . . .

Stafford was belabouring on the door opposite.

"The papers!" snapped Bellamy, still gazing down from the window. "Any papers in this house that are writ on———"

"Yes?"

"Burn them."

"Now?"

"This instant."

The young spy Swift did not go to the front door in answer to the knocking. Instead he looked furtively through the window.

What he saw sent him racing for the back door. He drew the bolts, flung it wide—and hurled himself into the arms of a captain and four sturdy patrolmen.

Those at the front of the house did not wait long. "It will take too long to kick the door down," said Stafford to the captain. "Break in a window."

The captain obeyed the order, using the butt of his carbine. Then he, with two of his men, remained outside while

Adkins, Stafford and the other two climbed through into the house. They were in time to meet Swift, whom Adkins recognized, in the grip of his captors and being forced back into the house through the back door.

"Where is the lady?" It was the detective's first question, ejected from his lips like a pistol shot, his eyes blazing.

"What lady?"

"Do not be impertinent. Miss Hart of Merton."

"You must have taken leave——"

"Answer my question." It was an order, a shout that rang in the back lobby of the house like echoed pain.

"There is no lady here."

There was a finality to the words, yet Adkins would not believe them. In his anguish he spun round on Stafford, cracking his cane against his own shin with a force fit to break it, forgetting all the courtesies in the framing of his request. "Search the place, every nook and cranny," he snapped.

"Aye," said Stafford, who had heard whispers of the thief-taker's association with the lady, and at this moment now knew them to be very true. Without another word he took two men and began to ransack the house.

"Why did you take her?" Adkins turned again to Swift, the tip of his cane quivering like an accusing sword-point at his throat. "What did you want of her?"

The young spy was now composed, his face utterly expressionless. Suddenly it was to him like a time towards which he had been trained over many years, a time when the future was blank and empty and somehow strangely meaningless.

"I do not know anything about the woman you speak of," he said, stubbornly, his voice hollow. "I know nothing of any woman."

"We shall see about that," said Adkins, "when we get you to Bow Street." He had regained control of his emotions, and suddenly he changed the nature of the interrogation. "You are a Frenchman, are you not?"

"Why, sir, I am English."

"You are a Frenchman."

"I am English."

"Then you have sympathies for France, eh?"

"You must be mad."

"That is not an answer to my question. Kindly answer it."

"I think it was an answer. If you think I am a Frenchman, or that I am for France, then I say with respect, sir, that you must be mad."

"We will extract a better answer than that, too," said Adkins, "when we get you to Bow Street."

In the house across the way Bellamy had gently opened the casement. He and Justice crouched beside it, each with a pistol in his hand. Behind them the glow of the burning papers was dying.

"Let us go," said Justice. "Every minute is more dangerous."

"No," muttered Bellamy. "I want to see what happens."

Over in Swift's lodgings Stafford returned to the thief-taker. "There is no woman in this house," he said. "There is no person at all."

"Are you—sure?" asked Adkins, and his voice was very low.

"Positive. We have turned the place upside down."

The detective treated the prisoner to a long glare. "I shall make you tell," he said.

Handcuffs were then fastened on Swift's wrists. "Let us be off, then," said Adkins.

Across the way the two spies saw the front door open and the party from Bow Street emerge with their prisoner.

"Mr. Justice," said Bellamy, very calmly, "shoot Mr. Swift."

"Shoot him?"

"Shoot him dead."

"Why?" Justice breathed the word incredulously.

"It is the only way to make *quite* certain that the young fellow does not talk."

147

"I—I can't," said Justice, lowering his pistol. "He—will not—talk."

"We cannot take the risk," snapped Bellamy, and his voice was very cold. "If he does talk our sacred mission is doomed. But it must not fail. It will not fail. There is only one thing that matters—and that is La Belle France. God save our emperor Napoleon."

As he spoke he was levelling his pistol and taking careful aim, and Justice, who had spied for France for many years, was white and nerveless.

Le Capitaine le Vicomte de St. Remy, fanatical soldier of France, worshipper of Napoleon, was a crack shot. When he pulled the trigger his own youthful comrade fell to the cobbles as the explosion still echoed in the narrow square.

The young spy lay on his back in the gutter, a wisp of fair hair blowing in the breeze. He was dead before Adkins, kneeling beside him, had ascertained the fact.

Swift had a moustache the ends of which pointed upwards, and in the gathering dusk it gave to his face the appearance of a smile.

To the detective it was like a smile of triumph, for there were certain vital things that he could not now wring out of him.

CHAPTER EIGHTEEN

Mr. Day's pistol was in his hand almost before the young spy's body had slumped into the gutter. The next second his arm jerked upwards and he was aiming the weapon, for from his position at the corner of the square he had seen the window from which the shot had come, for it had been briefly lit by an unmistakable flash.

His own shot following instantly on the other, echoed loudly within the enclosed buildings. It shattered the open casement. Glass tinkled to the cobbles.

It did not harm either Bellamy or Justice, who had withdrawn from the window and were now wrenching open the door of the room and pounding down the stairs. It did, however, mark for the others the house of the assassin.

Still kneeling beside the dead man, Adkins looked up at the window. "That house——" he shouted. "Break open that house——"

Stafford, too, was shouting orders. Already one of the two captains was at a lower window, smashing it inwards with the butt of his carbine.

"Seal the rear of the house," ordered Stafford, and the other captain, choosing one of several alleyways at the side of the square set off down it followed by his four men.

Down another clattered Day, who had mounted at once. Moving towards the square were also his own men, who had taken the two shots to be the signal for doing so.

In the house, the two spies had already reached the back door. Now they were racing down a narrow lane to the point where they knew Jamieson would be waiting with the horses.

Having not laid seige to this house but to the one opposite, the patrolmen did not know which lanes and alleys led quickly to the back of it, and they reached the rear door in time to see their colleagues, who entered at the front, bursting out of it empty-handed.

The horse patrolmen were riding down different lanes to converge on the square, as they had been told to do if they heard a pistol discharged. Day met two of them, and cried out to them to wheel around and make for the main street, near which they had been stationed originally.

Had they stayed where they were they would no doubt have cut off the spies' retreat. But as it was Ludgate Hill was unguarded as the escaping men rode out into it and swept down its short length unmolested.

Day heard the clatter of their hooves and turned his horse's head in the general direction of the sound, followed by two of his men. But they had to negotiate a number of narrow lanes and corners, and when they reached Ludgate Circus their quarry were nowhere to be seen and there were three different ways they could have gone.

The conductor halted his men. He must decide quickly which street to take. Had the escaping men chosen to hide away in the labyrinth of Whitefriars? If the patrol chased off there they would but lose themselves in the maze of squalid streets. Had they made for open country to the south, where a horse could be put to the limit of its speed?

Suddenly there was the bang of a fire-arm being discharged. The explosion echoed in the evening air and appeared to come from a point straight ahead down Fleet Street.

Day put heels to his horse and sped forward, followed by his two patrolmen. They were half-way down the Strand when they came upon the man who had fired his carbine.

He was a member of the foot patrol, and with him were two colleagues. He was bending over a crumpled human figure, and some little distance away a horse lay on its side.

The man was dead. His name, though they did not know it, was Jamieson.

"Bow Street horse patrol," called the conductor, reining in his horse.

From the distance ahead came the echo of horses' hooves. "Keep on after them," he said to his two men. "Try to keep within sound of them. I'll be after you in a moment."

They rode on while Day addressed the man with the carbine, raising his voice over the noise of the hooves. "Day's the name. Quickly, man—what happened?"

"Captain Higgins, of the foot patrol," came the reply. "There were three o' them, Mr. Day. Riding fast. Very suspicious. I called on 'em to halt and when they rode on I fired a shot at the legs o' one o' the horses, bringing it down. The rider lay stunned."

Day, still in the saddle, looked down. "This man was not killed by the fall," he observed, sharply. "He has been shot through the chest."

"I know, sir," replied the captain, "and in the name o' God, sir, it was astonishing. The other two halted and one o' them levelled a pistol at me. But when he saw my two men running up—they were patrolling nearby—he turned the pistol instead on this fellow as he lay stunned. His own man, I reckon, and he killed him in cold blood."

Again Day looked down at the inert figure. "The devil he did," he exclaimed, "and the second time this night, I'll be bound."

"Don't understand it, sir," continued the patrolman, leaning on his carbine. "Think you he had only one pistol, and when he saw my men running up he saw that his friend would be taken in any case, even if he shot me?"

"There is no time to talk of it, captain, and even less time to think. Take the body to Bow Street. Report in full to your Mr. Stafford. Ask that he tell Mr. Adkins, and please to say I have gone on after the two fellows. God grant I catch up with them."

With the words the conductor was off, spurring along the Strand in the gathering shadows, following the sound of his men, whom he could still hear, and cursing the coming of night, for in its darkness he would have less chance of running down the two men he sought, even though he had more than an idea what each looked like and, if Adkins was correct, the name of one of them.

He made by instinct for Wimbledon, for if it was not to Whitefriars the fugitives ran then it might be that other area with which they now associated some as yet unknown devilry they referred to vaguely as The Plot.

His was a fine blood horse, and thudding down the Brompton Road he overtook his two colleagues.

"They must pass our patrols," he yelled as he drew level with them, the wind plucking at his words, "do they keep to the road."

Day rode on ahead of his colleagues, putting his thorough-bred animal to the crop as well as the spur, knowing that they who sped so urgently from the law would not spare their own mounts.

The sound of those he chased was now lost in the night wind. But before he crossed the Thames into Putney he could make out in the gloom ahead the figure of a horseman riding hard in the same direction. As he gained on the man he became aware that he was dressed in a familiar uniform. One of his own men, he must have been patrolling this stretch of road when something had happened to set him to the gallop.

As Day drew level the patrolman did not at first recognize him, dressed as he was in civilian clothing.

"Day," he shouted, cupping a hand to his mouth.

"Sir," came the reply. Then, in explanation: "Two men, sir. Riding fast. Didn't answer my hail."

Day's eyes were gleaming. "Good man," he shouted. "I'm on the right road, then?"

"Aye, sir," was the reply, as side by side and in silence they settled in to their pursuit.

The hill at Putney slowed their pace, and Day listened keenly.

But from ahead came no echo, and there was no sound

save their own pounding and the rush of air about their ears.

At the top of the hill the conductor drew rein. Darkness lay over the heath. The shadows did not move. In the breeze the leaves whispered. And the two he sought were as ghosts that vanished in the night. For in this wild wilderness, even in daylight, it would take a regiment to flush them out.

The other two patrolmen came up, and the four horsemen stood together in silence for a time. Then Day found himself staring at the glow from the windows of an inn. Why, yes, the *Green Man*! It was an inn where much had happened already. An inn where he had run to earth a certain Mr. Jeremiah Bickershaw . . . and Mr. Bickershaw had had some very mysterious dealings with those the patrol now sought.

The conductor sent one of his men to guard the back of the inn. "Ask the ostler if he has a couple of winded horses in his charge," he ordered.

Another of his men was set to watch the front of the inn. The third he asked to follow him as, striding through the door, he shouted loudly for the landlord.

The man came, bowing and simpering, and Day was not over polite with him. He remembered that he had not liked the sly, smiling, thin-faced individual. He did not, for that matter, like any of the breed, for he had learned that many of them conspired with the highwaymen.

"Have any strangers come to this inn?" asked the police officer.

"Strangers, sir? We get 'em times."

"I do not doubt it. But this quarter hour?"

"No, sir. Oh, very definitely not, sir. No, sir."

Day swept an arm towards the men who sat at their ale. "Are all these—er, known to you?"

"Aye, sir. Not a one more'n a ten-minute walk or ride away. All reg'lars as you might say, sir."

Day addressed himself to the assembly. "Has anyone seen two men riding this way, and hell bent about it?"

There was a murmuring and shaking of heads.

"Or heard horses ridden hard?"

The replies were again in the negative.

"Landlord, I am looking for two men. I can describe them to you with some accuracy. May I take your word that they are not here, or do I have to ask to search your inn?"

"You may ransack every corner, do you not believe me. But I am most hurt, sir, at your manner."

"Cast back your mind, landlord. There was a night—and not long past—when I found here a man I wanted. You were not aware of his presence on that occasion, eh?"

"You are most unkind, sir."

"Perhaps so. But the two men I seek, they are not taking a turn at going to bed with your Miss Jolikin?"

"Sir!" The innkeeper's eyes were reproachful.

"Maybe I will take your word." Day was already turning as though to leave when abruptly he stopped speaking.

A door had opened at the rear of the inn, and the man who entered was Jerry Bickershaw.

"Mr. Bickershaw!" said the patrol chief, a gleam in his eyes answering the sudden smile on his lips. "Well met, Mr. Bickershaw, if I may say so."

The highwayman swept his hat mockingly. "Do not take me again, sir, unless this time you have a charge to prefer."

"What do you do here?" demanded Day.

"Lord save me," returned Bickershaw. "Can a man not go to an inn for his ale?"

"I am but interested that you should be here at this moment, Mr. Bickershaw. I have just chased two of your friends to this spot."

" 'Pon my soul, sir, I do not know of whom you speak, so I cannot say if they are my friends or not. If you can but say their names, or bring them before my eyes, then I might enlighten you. What say you, Mr. Policeman, eh?"

Day did not answer the highwayman. Instead he swung round on the innkeeper. "Landlord, I have changed my mind. I *will* search your place. Every room, sir."

154

As they strode from room to room, the stableman, interrogated by the patrolman in the yard, swore that no horses had been put in his charge these two hours or more.

"Aye, and those were cool and comfortable," he added, smiling as he fingered a coin in his waistcoat pocket. "Not been ridden a 'arf-mile, they 'adn't."

Because of that coin nestling comfortably in his pocket, the groom did not deem it necessary to mention that Mr. Bickershaw had returned this minute from taking two panting and sweating animals to the wooden hut in the orchard.

Day's search revealed nothing, nor had it been expected to because of Gentleman Jerry's air of boldness.

That assurance was due to the fact that the highwayman knew the inn as did few others, that he was confident that the entrance to the cupboard which formed a hiding-hole above the doorway was most skilfully concealed, and that as the men from Bow Street mounted and rode off an eye placed to a hole in the woodwork would be watching them go.

As Day had chased to Putney Adkins had not been idle. He traced and interviewed the owners of the two houses that faced each other across the little city square, the one where they had found Swift and the other where his murderer had lurked.

In the case of the former, the gentleman had only visited his property once since "the nice young man" had taken a lease on it four months previously.

Swift had turned up regularly at his home with the rent. No, he did not know anything about the young man, and he had never met any of his friends.

The house across the way was rented in the name of Stuart Jamieson, and the gentleman who owned it knew little more of any value to Adkins. The detective gave a description of Bellamy and Justice. "Have you ever seen such characters at the house?" he asked.

"I have not," was the reply. "I called once at the house

soon after he'd taken it. I thought my tenant lived there alone. I gathered that friends were visiting him but that they were in another room. I was not introduced to them and did not at any time see them. Mr. Jamieson always insisted that there was no need for me to call as he would bring the rent to *me*, which he did at regular intervals."

"Did you learn anything about the fellow, how he occupied his time, what his interests were?"

"He told me little of himself, save that he was a young gentleman of independent means."

"This, sir, may seem a strange question. Did you ever suspect he might be anything save an Englishman? A Frenchman, maybe?"

"Well, now you mention it, there *was* something a little odd about the young fellow," said the owner of the house. "He did not seem quite to be a Londoner. I could not place his accent, and sometimes I thought maybe he was a Scotchman, him having a Scotch name, sir. Once he made an exclamation in the French tongue, and when I observed that he could speak French he said he had learned the words in Scotland, where the dialect contained some words uncommon like French."

The owner of the house was asked to fulfil one more task —a somewhat unpleasant one. He was taken to Bow Street and shown the body of the man who had been shot in the Strand.

"Do you know this man?" asked Adkins.

"That," said the gentleman, "is Mr. Jamieson."

Long after midnight the thief-taker sat at his desk in the Bow Street office. His hands supported his head, and in the light of oil lanterns his face was long and pale. Still he had no lead, and still Rosemary was missing . . .

Over all the cases he had investigated in the past he had seemed to stand like a sort of presiding deity, looking in from afar with a passionless accuracy, like a calm and venerable philosopher. He had been as a man watching life and untouched by it, for always it had been others who had suffered robbery or death, and the criminal who would suffer also when he ran him to earth. His brain had worked, therefore, with an ice-cold precision.

But this time it was different. This time they against whom he pitted his wits had a woman in their grasp, and it was as though they had taken a part of his own heart and locked it away, and without it he was not a whole man to fight them. If they could shoot their own men to suit their devil's schemes, what would they not do to Rosemary?

What success would attend Josiah's pursuit of the bastards? Or what failure? Impatiently he waited for the conductor's return.

Day found him still sitting at his desk, immobile, trance-like, his eyes staring at the still flame of the lantern.

"Did you run them down?" asked the detective. His voice was dull, lifeless.

The patrol chief, knowing the reason for his friend's torment, glanced away from the look in his eyes. "I am very sorry," he said, gently. "I did not."

"Have you brought me—anything? Some clue?"

"I have brought you nothing, save that I chased them to the beginning of the Portsmouth Road. They could be off to the south coast. They could be making—for France, eh?"

The detective rose and paced the room. "I do not think so," he said, "for somehow I do not think they yet have the information they desire."

The sound of his measured tread on the bare boards was eerie in the dim and empty room. "I have gone over it all time and time again while you rode after them," he said. "I am now more than ever convinced they are spies, and that their mission is so important and desperate that they would rather murder their own comrades than risk that we might unseal their lips.

"I am sure it is they who have—taken Miss Hart. The fact

157

that they may have taken *her* means that they are uncommon interested in my Lord Nelson. 'Tis navy secrets they are after, I'm convinced. But what secrets, eh?

"Strange that it all began with thinking they but meant to break open Merton Place and commit a robbery. I did not dream they would steal—Miss Hart."

"Aye, 'tis strange."

The Little Ferret crashed a fist into his palm. "What do they want of our greatest admiral?" His voice was like a cry of pain. "If only we knew what they wanted it would help. But do we have any clues? Devil a one we have, friend. Devil a one."

CHAPTER NINETEEN

Rosemary Hart sank wearily on to the bed in the tawdry little room. For the twentieth time that day she had pulled and pushed at the door, only to find it firmly locked against all her efforts.

Apart from the narrow, iron bed and its soiled and rumpled blankets, the only other item of furniture was a hard, wooden chair, and on the floor in one corner rested a tin basin and a cracked, pot ewer containing washing water.

The one tiny window was glassless and securely boarded over, the pieces of wood so firmly nailed that they defied all her attempts to budge them. By standing on the chair, she had been able to peer through a narrow space between the timbers, but all she could see was row upon row of grey roofs and smoke curling from chimney pots. They were the roofs of Whitefriars, but this she did not know.

Several times she had put her lips to the wedge of daylight at the window and screamed for help. Each time the door lock had been turned, and a large, blowsy woman in a filthy apron and bonnet had entered, accompanied by a huge, dirty-faced, repulsive man. On each occasion the woman had dealt her a stinging blow across each cheek.

"Worse'n that y'll get," the slattern had shouted, "if yer don't keep quiet as a mouse."

This had not stopped her cries for help. Now she mounted the chair once more and put her face to the aperture between the boards.

"Help!" she yelled. "I'm a prisoner. Help! Help!"

The two slovens came in. This time it was the man who advanced towards her. About his body clung an evil odour; his thick lips parted in a sinister smile; a dirt-engrained hand clawed out towards her.

He grabbed her by a wrist and pushed her roughly on to

the bed. His foul breath sickened her as he leered at her from a bristly, unshaven face.

"Go a-shoutin' again, me beauty, and I'll come and make free o' your pretty little body," he rasped. "Gag yer I will, and 'ave me way o' yer." So saying he gripped the top of her dress and ripped it downwards.

Then the two went out, locking the door, their mirthless laughter ringing in her ears long after they had gone.

She did not shout again.

"The Lord save us," breathed the innkeeper as the patrolmen's hoofbeats died away. With trembling hands he clutched Bickershaw's tunic. "Get 'em out o' here," he pleaded. "Send 'em packing or I'll have an apoplectic."

"Don't be a fool," said the highwayman. "Those damned Robin Redbreasts may only be pretending to go away. S'pose they return? We'd all be for it."

The landlord's nervousness increased as the hour wore on. But at last Bickershaw got the two fugitives out of the hiding-hole.

"Off with you this minute," the innkeeper groaned at once. "Not have you in the place a second longer. Don't know who you are—and don't want to. A favour to Mr. Bickershaw it was and naught else."

But he stopped wringing his hands to accept payment for services rendered.

"One more favour," Bellamy asked of him. "Give us fresh horses in exchange for our own, for they are quite winded."

"I'll do no such thing," declared their unwilling host. "Your horses might be known. Might be a description out. Questions might be asked, and I've had enough o' questions for a long time to come. Now be off with you."

The highwayman brought the two weary horses from the shed. Then he took his own from the stable, mounted with the others, and moved out of the yard.

The world lay dead around them in the night as they clopped into the Portsmouth Road. There was no wind to whisper in the trees, and the silent ceiling of branches over-head made the spies' way darker than the dark.

In the last hours much had happened to them, and none of it had been in their favour. Things had been done, and had had to be done, that had shaken even the dedicated Justice, who did not lack courage, and left him white and drawn. He rode with his chin almost resting on his breast and his shoulders sagging.

But not so Bellamy, for he sat his horse erect and firmly. Despite what he had done, and what he still would do, his eyes flashed in the dark. Justice glanced at him and decided that he was some super devil.

"We must have fresh horses," snapped the spy chief.

"That," said Bickershaw, "is what I'm about."

Within a few minutes he led into the yard of the *Telegraph Inn* and roused the stableman, who did not boast a lively intelligence and was prepared to do whatever Bickershaw asked of him. As the man took charge of the tired animals and saddled two fresh ones, Bellamy stood in the straw and held council. He spoke in undertones so that the ostler would not hear.

"I would like to know what stir there is in town," he said to Bickershaw. "Who can I send to read the posters, for posters there will surely be. You see, Mr. Bickershaw, there have been two murders in town."

"I will go," said the highwayman.

"You will not go. I do not want you staring at notices in Bow Street. You are already associated with two men who fled from Ludgate Hill. I heard from the hiding-hole what the officer said. No, Mr. Bickershaw, you are to stay in these parts until I should want you. Never fear, I shall require your services.

"My friend and myself are making for the coast, where we shall hide out for a few days. We have to—er, reorganize our affairs. Why yes, I know the man to use. That fellow Jumper—he who calls himself Mr. Jack and is shy of his second name. He lives hereabouts. Can you contact him?"

"He comes to the *Green Man*. In any event, I know in whose household he works—that of a Mr. Pringle."

"Well, please to get him to journey at the soonest to Whitefriars. He will know where to find Mr. Speed. He is to tell him not to try to find Mr. Swift or Mr. Jamieson, but to lie low until he hears further from me. I am going to the coast now to make arrangements.

"Afterwards, Mr. Jack is to wander around Bow Street, read the posters about the murders and listen to the gossip in the *Brown Bear* opposite the police office. When he has acquired such information as he can pick up he is to acquaint you of it and you are to ride to me with it. You will find us, or word of us, at an inn called *The Seabird*. They tell me it's as lonely a place as ever a man did see, but you should find it quite easily, for another mile would take you to the coast at Dungeness."

"I understand."

"You will do as I say?"

"Aye."

"Excellent. Come, Justice."

They turned their horses' heads away from London and settled into a steady trot. Making for the south east, they had ridden out of Surrey into Kent, and put many miles behind them before the dawn came. In its eerie light they skirted Tunbridge Wells and cantered onwards for the sea.

Justice had ridden for long with a deep frown darkening his brow. "When will it be *my* turn to be murdered at your hand?" he asked at last. He had passed with each mile through varying emotions, but his voice was hollow now.

"I fancy it will never be your turn, for you are a real professional, Mr. Justice, and you have your wits about you."

The old spy replied without a glance at his companion. "I have my wits, 'tis true, but I'm thinking no man is safe in your hands. Aye, and no woman, either, now that you have that Miss Hart in your clutches."

"Since you mention it," said Bellamy, his voice as cold as the dawn, "no woman either."

For a time Justice did not speak again, but in the growing light his brow remained dark. "I have worked in exile in this country for a considerable time," he said, "and, *sacré bleu*, I have not yet found the need to kill."

"There was need tonight," snapped Bellamy.

"I wonder."

"I do not wonder. I know. My mission, as you well know, is a desperate one. Desperate measures are required. I think I must warn you, *mon ami*, that if ever it *were* necessary to turn my hand against you, then I would do it—for France."

"I do not think so," said Justice, calmly. "My knowledge of this country is vital to you."

The keen edge of Bellamy's voice was blunted. "*Mon ami*, it is a matter of how much one loves *La Belle France*."

"Of my love for France there is no doubt," said Justice, quietly and firmly, and his words put an end to the conversation.

They came to *The Seabird* at the breakfast hour, and Bellamy, who had not seen it before, thought it the most desolate inn he had ever seen. Justice, of course, knew it well, for it was the place where they met the smuggler and gave him messages for France.

It lay on a rise of the moorland road, as though it had slept for years . . . and was still sleeping. In the grey light it looked quite deserted, forlorn and haunted, as though it existed only in dreams. It would look better at night, thought Bellamy, with a lamp at its windows; but at night, no doubt, the shutters would be closed, as most of them were closed now . . .

The sign, bearing a painting of a white gull, creaked in the wind. The noise accentuated the loneliness of the old inn. And very solitary it was, for there was neither house nor hut around it as far as the eye could see. There was neither tree nor bush nor hedge either up or down the road, and any who approached might be seen for miles.

Onwards, over the rolling road, there was a glimpse of the cliff tops—and the sea.

"Now we are here," said Justice, drawing rein, "may I know your present plans?"

"Certainly, *mon ami*," replied Bellamy. "We shall remain for a few days. Here we can draw breath, for the Redbreast Patrol does not come so far. Indeed, for that reason, it might serve as a better headquarters. It is a good thing also that we come here when we do, for I am running out of money and we can send to France for more English currency when the next smuggler sails."

Turning in the saddle to survey the bleak countryside, he screwed up his eyes against the wind.

"The place gives me another idea, too," he said, and a slow, evil smile was spreading across his face. "We shall have the girl brought here, eh? 'Tis the very spot to keep her—until we decide what to do with her."

CHAPTER TWENTY

THE man known as Jack visited young Mr. Speed at the *Surrey Stingo*, delivered his message, then made for Covent Garden and Bow Street. Outside the police office he studied a number of notices nailed to a board. One of them took his interest, and he read it carefully. It stated:

TWO FOUL MURDERS

On the evening of 5th August, 1805, Two Foul Murders were perpetrated in the Citie, one verie near to Ludgate Hill and the other not far away att The Strand.

In connexion with the foregoing Crimes the Chief Magistrate's Officers are anxious to interview Two Male Persons, who they think may be of verie great assistance in Certain Inquiries att present being made by the said Officers.

One of the said Persons is a man of approximately thirty years of age or more, six feet in height or nott verie far short of it, and of slim and erect build. He has a rather thin face, a pale, smooth complexion, and dark and piercing eyes, with dark hair, verie dark and profuse eyebrows, a long thin nose of arched appearance and a large, black moustache of a type worn by The Military.

Jack Jumper stopped reading for a moment and fingered his chin. Unconsciously, he glanced around as though he feared he may be watched. It was, he knew, as fine a description of Bellamy as could be written down. What he did not know, however, was that its author was a man who had trained his mind to observe and retain the smallest and most inconsequential details.

The notice continued:

The other said Person is a man some four inches smaller and of slightly heavier build. He is clean-shaved, of a sallow but fine complexion, and his face is of somewhat broader appearance. His lower lip is thick; he has two moles, one on the left cheek near to the eye and the other at the right side of his chin. He is not of such grave countenance as his companion.

If the former were a description of Bellamy, decided Jumper, then the latter could be no other than Justice.
The notice ended:

Both are accustomed to wearing gentlemen's clothes, and it is suspected that although their speech is of good English they may sometimes be heard to have a slight foreign accent.
Any Person recognizing these two are requested to inform this public office at the soonest.

The servant from Wimbledon crossed the street and entered the *Brown Bear,* where for a long time he sat pondering over a tankard of ale. If Messrs. Bellamy and Justice had committed two murders, then he was not at all sure that he should continue working for them. And what was this mention of a foreign accent? Avarice and caution were present in equal parts in Mr. Jumper's character.

Suddenly he rose, went out of the tavern and hurried back towards Whitefriars and a further talk with Mr. Speed.

"I was to read some murder notices in Bow Street so as your friends would know wot was set down," the servant told him. "Why are they interested in such murders?"

" 'Tis but an academic interest, I'm sure."

"A wot?"

"Well, as you already know, Mr. Bellamy is writing a learned treatise on love and the making of love. Possibly he forgot to tell you that he is interested also in other aspects of human nature. Crime, for instance."

Jumper was smiling. "Do you think as I took in all that

rubbish? I didn't care much wot you was up to. I did, o' course, care about the money. But if they've done murder, then I draw the line at that."

"Why do you think they have committed murder?"

"In the first place, how did they know of the murders so soon? And why do the Bow Street officers want to 'ave a word wi' 'em?"

"Are they *named* in the notice?"

"To me as good as named. Descriptions fit 'em like fine clothes."

"You must not worry, Mr. Jumper——"

"Hold yer tongue. Haven't I said as 'ow you've never to speak of my name, not ever, and specially not now when there's talk o' murder?"

"I beg your pardon, *Mr. Jack*. Is that better?"

"Aye, Mr. Speed, much better."

"As I was saying, Mr. Jack, you must not be concerned."

"But I am. Notice speaks o' a foreign accent. I likes a bit o' business, but not wi' foreigners——"

"Do not be ridiculous, Jack. They are not foreigners."

"Aye, so *you* say. I don't like it. Not a bit, I don't."

Speed forced a laugh. "Your idea is preposterous. Now be off about your business. But first, tell me how you were to send this word to my friends?"

"Through Mr. Bickershaw."

"I see. Farewell, Mr. Jack."

As the visitor was disappearing through the door, Speed was already reaching for his hat and gloves. Cautiously he began to follow Jumper, who made his way back to Bow Street. From a doorway he watched the servant studying the notice again. Then the young spy blinked and whistled softly. Jack Jumper had pushed open the police office door—and disappeared inside.

Speed moved over to the notice and studied it. What did it mean? Why had he received orders not to look for Swift and Jamieson? Suddenly he became worried. Turning on his heel, he began to walk swiftly towards Ludgate Hill.

As he entered the little square he saw two men pacing the cobbles. One was outside Swift's lodging, the other at the door of Jamieson's. Without pausing, he passed through the square and down an alley beyond, catching a glimpse as he did so of the shattered casement above.

Meanwhile, at the desk inside the police office Jumper was engaging the attention of a clerk.

"The notice outside about—er, about the murders," he announced, and then ran out of words.

"Yes, sir. The notice about the murders."

"Yes. Er, the two men you want to speak to."

"Yes, sir. What about them?"

"Well, I was just interested. It says as 'ow they speaks a bit foreign like."

"Do you know any who answer the description, sir?"

"No. Not at all. Not that, sir. Not that at all, sir. I just wondered if they was foreign gentlemen."

"The notice says merely that they might sometimes be thought to speak like foreigners."

"I see," said Jumper, not seeing at all. "Can I ask—er, can you tell me—is there a reward for any wot can give information concerning the two gentlemen?"

The clerk laid his pen carefully on the counter. "As to that, sir, I do not really know," he said, smiling. "If you will take a seat, sir, I will endeavour to find out for you."

The clerk disappeared into a room behind the counter, closing the door behind him. "Mr. Adkins," he said, urgently. "A character has called asking if there is a reward for information of the murderers but does not admit to any knowledge of them. Seems a bit jumpy, too."

Without himself being seen, the thief-taker opened the door a few inches and peered through the aperture towards the counter. "The little fellow in grey with a red neckerchief?" he whispered.

"That's him," replied the clerk.

Quietly, Adkins closed the door. "Keep him in conversation while I leave by the back door," he ordered. "I wish

168

to know where he lives. No doubt he will not tell—or he may give a false address. Tell him that any reward would depend on how useful his information proved."

The clerk returned to the counter. "I have made inquiries for you, sir," he told Jumper. "The magistrates might consider giving a reward, but only if information given by any person led directly to the two men we wish to interview."

"Are they the murderers?"

"Ah, not so fast, sir. The notice does not say so, does it now?"

"Well, they're mixed up in it, eh?"

"Maybe so. Well, sir, have you any information?"

"Oh, no. Not at present."

"I see. However, as you have shown interest in the notice, perhaps you would care to leave your address, sir. You might be of some help—sometime."

"No, I won't say where I live."

"Perhaps you will give your name, then?"

"No, nor my name." Jumper was backing from the counter.

"Very well, sir. Thank you for calling. Good-day, sir."

"Good-day."

As Jumper left the office, Adkins, standing outside the front door, pretended to stumble and stretched out his hands as though to save himself. The little servant was bowled over in the dust.

"My humblest, sir," the detective apologized, helping the man to his feet and dusting him down. Then the officer beamed suddenly and pumped the man's arm.

"By Jehosophat!" he exclaimed, genially. "If it isn't my long lost cousin. Back from the Americas, eh, and never a word o' coming home."

Jumper, already pale and uneasy before the fall, was now shocked and trembling.

"Come," cried the Runner. "A drink for old time's sake." So saying, he put his arm firmly about the fellow's shoulders and propelled him across the street towards the *Brown Bear*.

169

"Could use—a drink," stammered Jumper. "That I could."

In the tavern Adkins plied the man with drink, admitted that he had been mistaken about the cousinship, swore that nevertheless he and his relative were as like as two peas, and kept up such a patter of gay conversation that little Jack Jumper was soon in danger of becoming quite tipsy.

In the company of the much-smiling, laughing, talkative Adkins, he recovered his confidence and was completely disarmed. With each drink he was growing in stature, and so often assured the detective that he was "in a good way of business" that momentarily he believed it himself and almost forgot that he was employed as a servant.

"I must be on my way," he said at last, realizing suddenly that his employer, for whom he had come to London to make a purchase, would not expect him to linger too long in the city.

"Just so," agreed Adkins. "Where do you live, my friend?"

"Wimbledon."

"Wimbledon!" the Runner cried in astonishment. "Well, if that ain't a coincidence. Damme if I ain't going there myself. I have a carriage and pair awaiting this minute, and you are most welcome to accompany me. Pray allow me the pleasure of your company."

Jumper, who was not too drunk to realize that by accepting he could pocket the fare his employer had given to him, agreed readily. Neither was he sufficiently inebriated to give his full name as they bowled along towards Wimbledon.

"You are a splendid fellow, and I must know your name."

"Jack."

"Jack what?"

"Jack, I said."

"Ah, I understand. *Mr.* Jack."

"If you like," grinned Jumper, winking and tapping his nose with a forefinger. "If you like."

The Runner, sitting benignly in the phaeton, twirled

his cane. "Let me know where I may set you down," he drawled. "I shall take you to your very gate."

"Not at all. Lay me down anywhere hereabouts."

"Nonsense! I will take you to your house."

"I would rather not, if you don't mind. We are almost there. If you stop now, eh?"

Adkins slapped his shin with his cane. "Just the place. Halt, driver, if you please. Here is an inn. I will buy you one more drink for friendship."

"If you don't mind——"

"Won't take 'no' for an answer. Wager you've had a few in that inn?"

"I have."

"Come, then."

Inside, the immaculate Adkins, at pains to drop a tankard to draw the landlord's attention to both himself and his companion, was careful not to let any of the contents spill on his clothes. He was profuse in his apologies to the inn-keeper.

He bade farewell to the so-called Mr. Jack in the doorway, with the intention of following him on foot. But the man had not taken twenty paces before he greeted another walking in the opposite direction. The two talked urgently, and Adkins drew further back in the porch. For the man who had just appeared was that footman from Merton named Stickles.

After a time the two walked off together, and the Runner went back into the inn and engaged the landlord in conversation.

"What a delightful fellow I took a drink with just now," he said, casually. "Only had the pleasure of his company for a few minutes. What is his name, eh?"

"That be Jack Jumper," explained the innkeeper. "Servant in the household o' Mr. Jonathan Pringle, o' Four Lanes 'Ouse. It's a step down the road on the left. Myself, I always thought he was a funny little feller."

Returning to Bow Street, Adkins sat in the phaeton

smiling in the afternoon sunshine. What had Stickles to do with his man? Why was little Mr. Jumper interested, and not a little anxious, about the two murders? Maybe he would soon know the answers to such questions, for he knew now where to find him, and when he did so—why, the pretentious little servant may not find him quite so friendly.

CHAPTER TWENTY-ONE

GENTLEMAN JERRY was riding the same road that two others had taken on the night of the murders. He bore the message that had been requested and one that had not. For Jack Jumper had scarcely reported to him and left when young Speed had arrived, grim-faced and much troubled, and with a warning on his lips.

The latter's visit was entirely to do with the alarming behaviour of Mr. Pringle's surreptitious servant. "Do not forget," Speed had said. "Say he is not to be trusted."

Bickershaw came to *The Seabird* in the fading light. He saw it black and gaunt on the rising plain, and before a single lantern had been lighted. It had the strange look of a place where no man lives, where ghosts and spirits abide in his place. The sea wind moaned, defying summer, and the darkening road, empty for miles, was more lonely than ever because of this solitary inn. The highwayman, who was not given to fancies, shuddered as he drew rein.

When he rapped on the door he raised only the echoes, and he began to wonder if it were an inn that did not care very much for customers—and not at all for strangers. But he had ridden the lonely miles, and had no wish to be locked out in the night. He set up a ceaseless knocking with the handle of his whip.

At last there was a sign of life, a shuffling tread from within and a voice that was unwelcoming. "I'm a-coming. Leave orf, damn yer. I'm a-coming."

The door creaked open to reveal a dark figure holding aloft a lantern which had just been lighted and whose flame flickered in the draught. In its glow Bickershaw made out the hulking figure of a man. He was ungainly, unsavoury, ill-dressed, a strange sort of fellow to be receiving him. The light fell on huge sea-boots instead of neat, clean shoes, on leather jerkin and frayed neckerchief.

"Waken the dead, you will," he growled. "Wot d'yer want, eh?"

"Is this *The Seabird*?"

"Aye."

"I've come to see Mr. Bellamy and Mr. Justice."

"Well, you've come to the wrong place. We ain't got no one o' that name." The man was closing the door on the visitor.

But Bickershaw's boot was inside, clamping down on the stone-flagged floor and preventing the door from shutting. "Open up!" he commanded, "or I'll blow your brains out!"

The oak swung back again and he entered unbidden.

"I've come all the way from London Town," he roared, "and I'll not be put off by you or any other scurvy fellow. This is the place they told me to seek, and what's more, sirrah, they're expecting me this minute. Now off with you, and bring me better information than you've offered up to now."

Muttering, the man slouched off, returning in a few minutes to grumble: "Only doin' wot I wus told, but if yer honour will come along o' me."

The highwayman was led up a dark and rickety stairway, which creaked at every step, to a dark landing where a chink of light showed where a door stood ajar. On this the man tapped hesitantly, then pushed it open at a call from inside.

Bickershaw entered an ill-furnished room lit by two candles, his boots echoing on bare boards. At a rough deal table sat the two he sought, scowling and ill at ease in the comfortless room. Before them lay paper and ink, and they lay down their pens as the visitor came in.

"Ah, Bickershaw," said Bellamy, "so you found your way here."

"Aye, but very near had the door closed against me," returned the highwayman.

"My apologies," said the spy, "but my orders to the fellow

were precise. He is not to admit of our presence—saving to those we wish to see. You will understand, of course, in the circumstances."

"S'pose I do really. I'm not asking what you're up to, but it's for no good, I'd wager."

Justice indicated a hard wooden chair. "Not led a blameless life yourself either," he said, "and don't forget we know it, should you ever be tempted to let your tongue wag about *us*."

"You can count on me," said the highwayman.

"We waste time, gentlemen," cut in Bellamy. "Now, sir, what do you have for us? Do you bear the information we require?"

"I have what you wanted—aye and more," declared the visitor. "Consequently, I think I may ask for double pay."

"If it is worth it." Bellamy turned to Justice. "Charles, in that which you have writ have you asked for more money?"

"I have."

"Good. Now, Mr. Bickershaw, I am all ears."

"Well, there are two descriptions out, and I'd say they fit you gentlemen like you stood before 'em while they wrote it down."

The visitor proceeded to give the details that had been contained in the notice in Bow Street.

"H'm" growled Bellamy. "They've almost got the number o' hairs in my moustache. Now how have they got so detailed a description?"

"The patrol that accosted us in the Strand?" suggested Justice.

"Nonsense. It was all over in a moment, and we had our backs to 'em before you could cock a pistol. No, Charles, there is someone who knows us better than we think. Now who could it be?" He paused. "Names?" he snapped then. "Any names given?"

"No names."

"For that, gentlemen, may the Mother of God be praised.

Charles, it would seem you must grow a moustache while *I* —why, *I* must shave mine off. We must lose no time in making ourselves vastly different persons. Now, Mr. Bickershaw, you say you have something else to declare?"

"I have. The information was got, as you suggested, by that bloody little hypocrite Jumper. Now I have something to say about *him*. Unknown to the little viper, Speed followed him back to Bow Street."

"For what reason?"

"Because he said he didn't like murder—nor working for foreigners."

The silence was tense. Bellamy sat very still. Justice rose abruptly to his feet.

"Continue," breathed Bellamy.

"Not much more to be said," declared Bickershaw. "Speed saw that bloody Jumper study the notices again—and walk into the police office."

Slowly, like a man grown suddenly old, Bellamy rose. His eyes smouldered. "Justice, you must parcel up my report with your own and see it safely to the ship. I shall not be there, for I have other work to do." He spoke softly, like a man in a dream. "First, I must shave my moustache and eyebrows and bleach my hair the colour of corn. I shall be riding back the way we came. I would send you, Charles, but I think you may be a trifle squeamish, and I would see the job done properly. Expect me back tomorrow."

He strode to the door and wrenched it open, his eyes flashing, his moment of apathy gone. "Hey, you there," he roared down the dark staircase. "My horse and my boots, and quick about it, or I'll have your old sea-legs."

Within the hour the *Capitaine le Vicomte de St. Remy* was mounted and away, clattering on the road that led away from the sea, disappearing into the night with only the moon for company.

When he had gone the seaman who had opened the door to Bickershaw came up to the room. "I'm off to the ship now," he declared. "I must sail soon or I'll miss the tide."

Without replying, Justice took the papers on which they had been writing from the table and stuffed them into a small pouch on a light, narrow belt. "Put it on—the usual way," he ordered.

The seaman took off his tunic, jersey and shirt, strapped the belt round his chest and put his clothes on again. Then he went out and began to descend the stairs.

"Come," said Justice to Bickershaw, and the two followed him from the inn.

They went on foot, for the cliff path was steep and narrow and no animal save a mountain pony could have descended in safety to the beach. The sea wind moaned and it was a desolate darkness. They trudged in silence, taking glimpses behind them though they knew that no one was there, and keeping close together as if they feared to lose human contact.

When they reached the cliff top they sensed rather than saw the sea, and when they began to descend to the lonely bay they picked their way warily on the dangerous path. Now and then a stone was dislodged and fell for a long time before its echoes came.

Threading their way through boulders and pebbles they could just discern the shadowy outlines of a small vessel anchored out in the bay. Across the sand two men waited with a rowing boat.

They addressed him as their skipper, and when they had launched the boat he splashed into the water and climbed into it.

"You know what to do," called Justice, as the oars dipped. "*Bon voyage* and safe return. We await what you bring back."

Soon the ship that sailed more at night than ever it did by day weighed anchor and moved out of the bay on a fair wind for France. Only when it had gone did Justice, shivering a little in the freshening breeze, turn to go.

"The oddest landlord you ever did see," he confided. "Keeps a ship as well as an inn, and he sails more than he serves ale. That is why he's as precious to us as a bag of gold."

"Why did you accompany him here?" asked Bickershaw.

"I must needs see him sail with my own eyes," was the reply.

Climbing the cliff path, Bickershaw said suddenly: "You are Frenchies, aren't you?"

Justice paused for a single moment. "We are what we are," he said. "Take your payment and ask no questions."

Late the next day Bellamy returned to the inn like a man who had ridden hard and long. His face was expressionless.

He asked no questions and offered no explanation of whatever might have befallen. He went to his bed and slept soundly all night.

The next day he gave an order to Bickershaw. "I think you should be on your way," he said. "You will find Mr. Speed at the *Surrey Stingo*. I want you and he to bring the girl here. I suggest a private coach, and one that is not open, for if need be you may have to bind and gag her."

CHAPTER TWENTY-TWO

To Jedd Stickles it was just another night in bed with Jenny the lady's maid. If it were anything more important than that, then perhaps it could also turn out to be part of his new business venture with one John Bellamy, who paid good money for what appeared altogether worthless information. That was, if the passionate Jenny had something to tell as well as give.

For the time being, however, the wanton footman gave himself up to unrestrained pleasure, quite unaware that before the dawn chill cooled their hot bodies he would be in possession of an item of intelligence that the strange Mr. Bellamy would regard as of the most exciting.

Meanwhile, Stickles and his bed partner were silent so far as speech was concerned, their association having reached a stage where it was somewhat difficult to say which was seducing the other.

The bed clothes began to slide, and Stickles was treated to a view of his mistress's naked body in the moonlight that filtered into the little room. When at last they began a languorous conversation they were in no mood to keep the merest secret from each other.

"Right hot bitch you are," mumbled the footman. "What a lass, eh? Fast as a fiddler's elbow."

"Didn't notice you grumblin' when we was——" Jenny did not finish her sentence, but gave him several meaning kisses on his neck.

"Daft little bitch," he said, affectionately, passing a hand over her cheek and twining his fingers in her hair. "I wasn't *grumbling*."

"Well, then?"

"I was just *saying* as how you're a hot little bitch. I wasn't saying as how I didn't like it."

"Oh."

There was a pause, during which both nearly fell asleep.

"Wonder what milady would think," murmured Stickles. "If she knew we was at it, I mean."

"She's no room to talk, 'er and 'er Lord Nelson. Wot a time they'll be 'aving to themselves w'en he comes 'ome. By the way, she's at it again."

"Who's at it?" Jedd's voice was sleepy.

"Milady."

"Oh." The footman yawned. "At wot?"

"Readin' 'er letters ter me. Bust she would if she didn't read out 'er letters. Started again today she did."

Stickles shot upright in bed. "That's wot I've been waiting for. That's wot he said. If Miss Hart was out o' the way——"

He rested back on an elbow, and leaned over towards the reclining Jenny, his warm chest brushing her breasts. His face was near to hers, his eyes gleaming. "Out with it, Jenny-o. Wot did the letter say?"

"It said milord was a-coming 'ome."

"The admiral?"

"Aye."

"When is he coming home?"

"On 'is way now. Letter was sent by fast despatch vessel. 'E was turnin' for 'ome then. There wus summat about little likelihood of a battle wi' the enemy fleet at the moment, and milord was given leave to sail 'ome while Admiral Cornwallis kept a watch at sea——"

"You've a good mem'ry, Jenny. I'll give you a kiss for it." He brushed his lips on her brow.

" 'Course I've a good mem'ry, but I want more'n a kiss for it."

"You'll get that, too, lass. But first, did milord say how long it would take?"

"Aye. Thought with fair winds he'd be off Portland by August 17th and be into Portsmouth by the following day."

Stickles leaned back on the pillows, pulling her on to his

shoulder. "Thank you, my love," he said. "Done me a great service you have."

Their lips were together again, but his mind was not now completely fixed on the business of making love. "Three days to go," he was thinking. "Just time to get word to Mr. Bellamy. The day—and the very port. Surely for that it would be a large silver piece for him, perhaps even a gold megg . . ."

He did not know, as his amatory fumblings re-commenced, that when he passed on the information he would be doing a great disservice to his country, or that time was running fast now for a man from France who was sworn to change the course of history.

Stickles was off before the dawn and battering on the door of the *Green Man* at first light. The innkeeper opened up cursing and pulling his night cap out of his eyes, allowing the footman entrance and closing the door against the morning mist.

"Where's Jerry?" he asked. "For Christ's sake, where's Gentleman Jerry?"

"In bed and not to be disturbed," replied the innkeeper. "Out late he was."

"In bed with Jessie Jolikin, eh?"

"Aye. Not in bed by 'isself, an' that's for sure. But if you disturbs 'im, I'll not answer for it. 'Arf kill you, 'e would."

"Don't think so," said Stickles, smiling. "I can make him some money I can—to buy Jessie a string o' beads."

With the words the footman was making his way towards Miss Jolikin's bedroom. He kicked at the door until Bickershaw's voice roared from within.

"Open the door," called the footman. "It's me, Jedd. Jedd Stickles."

Bickershaw opened the door naked save for a woman's nightgown hastily twisted round his middle. "Get to hell out of here, Stickles. I've only got to bed this quarter hour."

"It's urgent, Mr. Bickershaw. I've got h'a helluva

important message for you know who. Very private it is. Get the girl out o' the room."

"Can't, she's not got a stitch on," replied the highwayman.

"Well, close the door and I'll tell you here." Quickly Stickles told what the admiral had written. "And don't forget to tell him who told you," he added. "I've a feelin' for the gold meggs just as much as you."

"I'll ride at once," said the highwayman. "It's a long way, right down south to the sea."

"Where?" asked Stickles.

"Not far from Dungeness near the Romney Marshes," said Bickershaw. "But don't tell a soul or you'll have us both in damnation."

In just quarter of an hour he was on the road, settling his horse to a steady pace, grinning at the memory of the reproach and anger in Miss Jolikin's eyes, but smiling still broader at the thought of the money he would assuredly be paid.

In abducting Rosemary Hart the French killer had pulled off a far greater masterstroke than he could have imagined. For because of it Harry Adkins was not himself. Whereas in the past the thief-taker had always gone about his business with a cool head, his deductions were clouded now by emotion.

But at least he did not remain inactive. Day after day he went to the place he believed the likeliest for hiding anything or anybody—Whitefriars.

In old, worn clothes he trudged its narrow dingy streets. One by one he visited the unsavoury alehouses, lingering in the tawdry parlours to listen to the talk, telling the landlords that he was looking for his sister, who had run away from home.

If any of them had seen her they must surely have remembered, for the likeness he gave of her came straight from his heart; when he gave her description it was as though there hung before him a portrait of her painted by a master.

But always his question was met by the bleakest stare. Though he did not know it, there was a look in his eyes that somehow moved them, and they shook their heads as he went out.

"I'm looking for a woman . . ." In all the squalid little shops he uttered the words as he studied their wares and bought a trinket or two.

"Has a woman who is a stranger come to the district? Perhaps as a guest?"

They grinned. "A guest? That's a laugh. They ain't got enough bread for themselves around 'ere."

"Have you seen a lady dressed in pink silk edged with lace?"

They scoffed. "There ain't none o' the quality around 'ere."

In the alleyways and on the street corners he spoke to men, women and children, and he began to believe that it could be from the children he might gain a lead. But each night he went home weary and humbled.

It was both remarkable and distressing. He, the celebrated detective, the little ferret, could not find that which he sought for most.

Then, one day, a throbbing started inside his chest as he talked to an urchin and showed him a coin in his extended palm.

"Must've bin a lidy livin' in that room up there, but nobody never did see 'er," he heard the boy saying.

In the lad's begrimed face the blue eyes were clear and innocent, and Adkins pressed the money into his hand before he had finished interrogating him. "How do you know, lad, if you did not see her?" he asked, in a gentle, quavering voice.

"I 'eard 'er, I did."

"You *heard* her? *What* did you hear?"

The urchin wiped his nose on his sleeve, then scratched his tousled head to collect his thoughts. "I dunno wot I 'eard, sir, savin' that it were a voice like a growed lidy an' it were screamin' loud."

"What—was she—screaming? Please, my boy, try to remember."

The head was scratched again. "Dunno, sir. Honest, sir. It was just 'orrible like."

"Which window did it come from?"

"That one, sir. The one all boarded up."

"Thank you, my boy, thank you, and you must have another penny." Adkins was striding for the door beneath the high window.

It was opened by a big powerful, uncouth individual who towered above the smaller man, growling a query as to why he had been disturbed.

"You have a lady living here." It was a statement, not a question.

"I ain't."

"Do not lie, fellow. You have a lady living here."

"I ain't got nuffing o' the sort. 'Ere, you little bastard, I'll knock yer blarsted 'ead in——"

"Hold your tongue!" Adkins rapped out the words, and there was a keen edge to them.

By now it was dawning on this giant that the man before him had a speech that was not of Whitefriars and an inescapable air of authority.

"I wish to see who is in the room above," said the detective.

"I don't 'ave to let yer. I ain't never seen yer afore."

"No, you do not need to. But if you keep me out of this house it will go ill with you. I am from Bow Street—on the authority of the magistrates. Stand aside, sir, or I shall return with men of the patrol."

At that the man in the doorway blinked and moved backwards, while the visitor advanced resolutely.

"Quickly, man, show me to the room this instant."

The big man went up the rickety stairway, Adkins following, and pointed to a door. The detective almost hurled himself at it, wrenching the handle, and it opened easily. He nearly fell inside, but recovering his balance he looked quickly about him. It was certainly the room with the boarded window. It was dim and dirty. But, save for its pathetic scraps of furniture, it was empty.

It was as though some force within that forsaken room had dealt him a physical blow. For a moment he reeled back, his face ashen, his mouth agape. Then came his fury. It was unleashed in a great shout that echoed in hollow waves of sound along the musty corridor and down the dark, old stairs. "What have you done with her?"

For all his size the man on whom he turned was conscious of a force with which he could not deal. What spirit he had possessed drained from him. "It weren't me, sir. Honest, it weren't. It were *them*."

"Who?" demanded Adkins.

"Don't rightly know, sir. Never did know their names."

"Paid you, I suppose."

"Aye."

"Who brought her?"

"Two gentlemen."

"What were they like?"

The man was not capable of describing them. By questioning him, the detective found that the dead Swift could have been one of them, but that he had not returned with the two who had taken her away. Who were these two, then? All Adkins could discover, by giving further descriptions, was that neither Justice nor his saturnine companion, whose name he did not yet know, had ever been to the house.

"Where did they take her?" Adkins knew as he uttered the words that there would be no satisfactory answer to the question.

"Came in a coach for 'er. Forced 'er to go. Said as they'd not be comin' back ever . . ."

The villains had covered their tracks with professional efficiency. The man who had acted as Rosemary's jailer could throw no light on where any of them had lodged.

185

Just to make sure, the thief-taker rapped out a short description of Rosemary.

"'That was 'er,'" was the reply. "That was the lidy."

For Harry Adkins the trail had halted once more, this time in a tawdry, ill-lit room.

He felt very lonely descending the stairs and desolate tramping his way out of Whitefriars. He had a long way to walk, and this maze of streets and alleys was not the safest place in the city for an honest man, particularly if he were also a policeman. Moreover, the man he had just interrogated would already have raised an alarm that he was a Bow Street Runner.

It was not long before he heard a pair of footsteps following him. He did not look behind, but walked on steadily. Soon the echoes behind him increased. He who tailed him had been joined by others.

He paced on, outwardly calm.

It had been a reckless thing he had just done, but to him it had been also very urgent. The knowledge afforded him some control over his fear.

At last a crowd gathered behind him, but strangely kept its distance. In England an organized police force was still young; few liked it, least of all the denizens of Whitefriars. The tail he was gathering was a rabble of cut-throats, sneak-thieves, cutpurses and bridle culls.

Yet for the moment, oddly enough, none rushed forward to accost the defenceless figure. Perhaps they were still a little awed by his act of rashness—and his erect, strutting little figure.

Suddenly someone hurled a stone. It struck the wall beside him and rattled to the cobbles.

On he walked.

Behind him a pistol exploded. The shot was wide of its mark.

But he could no longer make a show of ignoring the mob. He darted into a long, dark alley, searching desperately for somewhere to hide. Before the crowd jammed in after him he had picked up a stone and hurled it forward so that its echoes came from the gloom ahead. Then, as he pressed himself into a dim alcove, the crowd jostled past him.

They went on, a shouting, cheering tide flowing out into the street beyond, while Adkins slipped back the way he had come.

Now he took to his heels, this man to whom in the ordinary way of things running was like a loss of dignity. He disappeared into a passage opposite, and raced out into another street.

Through the labyrinth he fled, and luckily he knew its secret ways.

Next, the Little Ferret nosed his way to Wimbledon, where the scent led to two people.

First he went to Merton Place. Jedd Stickles opened the door to him, politely asking if it was Lady Hamilton he wished to see.

"It is you," said Adkins, "whom I wish to see."

"Me?"

"Yes, Stickles, *you*."

"Lor', Mr. Adkins, sir, I am h'at a loss to know why."

"You will soon learn, Stickles. Pray take me to your room, where we may talk in private."

In the footman's small bedroom the detective eyed some articles of female underwear that had been thrown over a chair. "I notice you are married, Stickles," he observed.

"Married? Not a bit o' it, Mr. Adkins. Mind you, I'm not lonely o' nights. I don't go without. Have my fun o' the wenches. But marry 'em? No siree! There's no law against it, eh?"

"There is no law against it. But I did not come to discuss wenching."

"Pity, sir. 'Tis my favourite pastime."

"Do not, pray, be flippant with me." With the tip of his cane Adkins removed the underclothes from the chair and sat down upon it. "Now please to tell me how well you are acquainted with a certain Mr. Jack Jumper."

The footman's assumed confidence was deflated. "You said—er, Jumper?"

"You heard what I said. I'd trouble you for an answer."

"Scarcely know the man."

"Come, Stickles, you will have to do better than that. I saw you with my own eyes greeting him—and with some familiarity."

"Well, I can tell you the house to find him."

"You may spare yourself the trouble. I know where to find him, should I want him. I'd like to discover instead what you know about him."

"Let me see." Stickles tapped his forehead. "He is a servant at a household, much as I am. We frequent the same alehouses, and talk of our employers. We have something in common, so to speak."

"H'm, do you know of any reason why he should be interested in a notice at the Bow Street Public Office— *about murder?*"

"Lor' love us, I do not."

"Very well. If he should tell you anything at all about a murder, will you promise to inform me?"

"I will."

"Excellent."

As the thief-taker rose, the door of the bedroom opened. On the point of entering, the girl named Jenny stopped, a hand to her mouth.

"Oh, I didn't know——" she exclaimed.

"H'excuse me," said Stickles, drawing himself to his full height. "I'm talkin' to a gentleman."

Hurriedly, the girl left.

"If I am not mistaken," observed Adkins, "that is my Lady Hamilton's personal maid."

"She is. She's by way o' being a very special friend o' mine," boasted the footman, winking. "And there's no law against that, either."

188

"There is no law against that," agreed Adkins, smiling.

Leaving Merton, the detective was soon at the house where Jumper worked and lived and being shown in to Mr. Pringle, his employer.

"I should like your permission to interview your servant, Jack Jumper," announced the Runner.

"Why Mr. Adkins, you are a little too late," said Pringle. "If you would talk to *him*, then you must gain entry to the next world. For he is as dead as mutton. He has been missing for days, and he was found in my grounds this very morning, strangled to death. Murdered, sir—and the rope that did it lying beside him."

CHAPTER TWENTY-THREE

ADMIRAL LORD NELSON was coming home. He was, as he had reckoned, abreast of Portland Bill as daylight came on August 17th. At noon the Isle of Wight came into view, and at 1 a.m. the next morning his massive floating headquarters, the flagship *Victory*, and the accompanying *Superb*, anchored off Portsmouth.

But it was not until 7 p.m. on the 19th that he was given permission to come ashore, because there had been outbreaks of yellow fever at ports of Spain and Portugal and he had to persuade the authorities that he had not been in contact with the disease.

Bellamy and Justice, of course, were among the crowds that had packed every spot with a view of the harbour from the moment his flag had been seen at Spithead.

Having known almost as soon as the Admiralty and Lady Hamilton that he was on his way, and when he might arrive, they had stationed themselves in good time and had an excellent vantage point.

Each had two pistols hidden in the voluminous pockets of their greatcoats, and a keen observer among the laughing, joking throng might have thought the two somewhat ill at ease.

Never did England give a greater welcome to its famous admiral as on this historic August Monday. Always he had had the nation's admiration. Now, it seemed, he had its love.

As his barge came slowly in, and for long afterwards, the rain-wet streets and harbour echoed to resounding cheers. This pale, slight man of forty-six was as revered in England as he was hated by Admiral Villeneuve.

The two French spies took careful note of Lord Nelson as he stepped ashore, committing every detail to memory. He was an easy target, for he would be known anywhere.

For one thing, his uniform was emblazoned by his four stars of chivalry. And if he did not wear it his slim, weakly figure was instantly recognized by the green eye-shade and the empty sleeve.

Bellamy, who was nothing if not a good soldier, had a moment of high regard for the man.

"I have heard it said," he observed, "that fearful spinsters and old folk in England are terrified if he is not at sea, so great a confidence have they that he can save them from invasion."

But with the words his chin was firm and his mouth grim again. He put his hands in his pockets and gripped what lay there.

"You do not," breathed Justice, "intend to do it now?"

"Not unless I am so near to him that I cannot miss," whispered Bellamy. "If we did miss we should be surely caught, and the attempt would be over for good. No, I plan to do it in some comfort."

Lord Nelson went to the *George Inn* in the town's high street to order a post-chaise. The two Frenchmen followed, but the street was jam-packed and they could not get near him.

The admiral ordered tea while he waited for the carriage. Then, at nine o'clock of a wet night, he set off for Merton, unaware that two dark figures, mounting at this moment, would continue to trail him in the night long after the rest of those who followed his carriage so triumphantly had turned back again.

That night was notable for another event, and it had to do with his mistress's poor niece. For Rosemary Hart it was to be the most tragic night in her life.

The Seabird, where she was now locked up, was like a haunted place. The wind blew the rain-mist in from the sea, and its grey fingers took hold of the inn and seemed to lift it, dark and glistening in the wet, from its contact with earth.

Since Rosemary had been brought there both Speed and Bickershaw had shared the room, guarding her with their presence as well as the locked door. But this night the little smuggler was expected back from France, and Speed had made his way down to the beach with a lantern.

After he had gone the highwayman had kept glancing up at her. Now, over the rim of his ale tankard, he was staring at her lasciviously.

"You're a pretty 'un all right," he observed, his eyes narrowing.

"I do not thank you for the compliment. I would rather know how long you are to keep me here, and what is to become of me." Her spirited reply had the effect of further inflaming him.

"Now, now, my pretty, don't ask such leading questions, or I might have a mind to answer them. 'Tisn't for me to say, for I'm but a servant in the matter, but I shouldn't be surprised if they don't ship you off to France one o' these dark nights, and the Lord knows what'll happen to you there. On the other hand, they might just do away with you. Satisfied?"

She remained silent.

Bickershaw poured more ale in his tankard from a small keg he had brought up from the cellar. Already he had taken a large amount of the stuff.

Fixing his leer upon her, he gulped more, and some of it spilled down the sides of his mouth.

"I'd be thinking you've a damned pretty body under those skirts," he said.

"Please to keep your thoughts to yourself," she said. "I am not interested in them."

"Damme if I've not a mind to *make* you—er, interested in me." He rose unsteadily, belching. "You are unkind, ma'am, not recognizing I pay you a compliment. Biggest compliment of all—telling you that—that you're the most bedworthy little creature I ever did see."

"Hold your tongue," she said, fear growing. "You had

seemed to have some manners. Pray return to them."

He put the tankard to his lips again, emptying it. "So you think I'm not a gentleman, eh, my sweet?"

"If you were once, then you have sunk very low."

"Oh-ho, my little miss. Bit of a vixen, eh? Well, I like you the better for it. Let me tell you, ma'am, I'm a gentleman born. But very unfortunate I've been. You just don't know how unfortunate."

"If you continue annoying me, then I don't care either."

"Don't care? Don't care? Damme if I don't *make* you care! Prettiest wench I ever did see—and no gentleman could say fairer than that. The very sight o' you makes a man mad—that's if he calls himself a man—and ho, my beauty, you must damn well take the consequences. Have your body, I will, if 'tis the last thing I do. Give you the hottest tumble you ever did have."

He hurled the tankard aside, its rattling echoing from the boards, and lurched forward.

She backed to the furthest corner of the room, her eyes fixed on his red face and glowing eyes. He was still shouting, his lewdness increasing, but she could not hear his words any more, for it was as though her mind was shutting out his profanities. She could still hear the rattle of the discarded tankard, though it had long ceased to roll.

As she cowered, his hand shot out to the top of her dress, gripping it where it was full bosomed and partially revealing, and gave a mighty tug, tearing it downwards.

She scratched and kicked, but the leather of his high boots was hard and tough. She screamed, but there was no one to hear her . . .

Wriggling out of his grasp, she wrenched uselessly at the handle of the locked door. He came at her again, and she eluded his grasp, lifted the tankard from where it lay on the floor and hurled it at him.

But he caught her again in a corner, and dragged her to the floor. A knee on her chest, he produced a sharp knife and cut her petticoats and the strings of her stays. All she could hear was his hard breathing. All she could see was the light of lust in his eyes. She could not move as systematically he tore off her clothes. She prayed that the candles would go out.

On the floor her hand found the hard metal of the tankard that had crashed down. She gripped it and struck at his head.

Without a word he knocked it spinning from her hand. Then the room, and the flickering candles, and her whole world whirled into darkness and despair. She was ice-cold and yet burning, full of pain and horror and revulsion, sweating and faint. She felt she would suffocate.

Her finger tips found a space where the floorboards had come a little apart, and she drove them down into the aperture until her hands were tortured and bloody. . . .

When he let her go she rose unsteadily, shrinking against the wall. It was as though his act of premeditated cruelty had rendered her a dumb mute. She spoke to him only with her eyes, which were red, blinded by tears, accusing and full of reproach.

She crept slowly to the furthest corner, sliding down in it until she sat in a pitiful, dejected little heap, clutching her torn dress and draping it like a merciful blanket over her naked body.

He lumbered over to the table, where he found another tankard and filled it, and there he sat, very heavily and strangely silent.

In the corner Rosemary slumped pitifully. She thought of her Harry Adkins and his gentle smile. Harry Adkins, who had not yet taken her. Her eyes filled anew and the tears coursed down her face.

In a few violent, agonizing minutes she had been robbed of all her future. For if ever she escaped from this nightmare she knew with a deep and fatal understanding that she could never go back now to the man who had her heart in his keeping.

CHAPTER TWENTY-FOUR

LORD NELSON turned into the gates of Merton Place at six o'clock in the morning. It was a rapturous homecoming, and Lady Hamilton had already arranged many lavish dinner parties to show him off to everyone who may know him.

Lady Bolton had been invited, and all her nieces and nephews, and the Matchams were to come, and Lord Minto, and Mr. Perry, editor of the *Morning Chronicle*. Oh, and a host of relatives.

And there was to be one more guest, by special request of the Admiralty and Sir Richard Ford, of Bow Street— Mr. Harry Adkins. For the celebrated detective wished to talk to the admiral and mingle with his friends.

Home from the sea, the sailor was to preside at his long table with its crystal glasses and rich Worcester china decorated with the coat-of-arms of Viscount Nelson, Duke of Brontë.

He would revel in this, for he was a man who loved glory and spoke openly, not believing in secrets—even sometimes military ones. So the searching brain of Mr. Adkins might pick up the one clue that would knit together the mystery that surrounded this country house.

But before the first of those parties, on the morning after the admiral's return, Nelson set off to visit the Admiralty and afterwards Mr. Pitt.

When he left in his own coach with Lady Hamilton two gentlemen had made it their business to be taking a morning ride in the vicinity, and on this August day they trailed after him into London. It was unfortunate for them that the carriage did not take the road away from the city, for it was on that one Mr. Jeremiah Bickershaw had marked several convenient spots.

However, they watched the coach drop his lordship at the Admiralty, while Lady Hamilton went on to her little house in Clarges Street.

It was perhaps just as well that the time had not yet come, decided Bellamy, for the smuggler would be in by now, releasing Bickershaw to come to their assistance.

That evening the detective had a talk with the admiral, but gained no clue as to why any gentleman who was suspected of being a spy, and who had once assisted French prisoners-of-war to escape, should hope to derive any benefit from his personal letters or abducting Lady Hamilton's innocent little niece.

"Why, Mr. Adkins, they are entitled to learn anything they please about me or my family," said his lordship, cheerfully, "for my wild geese are all at sea, and the fellow of whom you speak must sail after them if he would learn our secrets."

Later, in the big drawing-room, Adkins took part in the conversation.

"Have you seen this new-fashioned thing called a railway?" asked the admiral's brother, the Rev. William Nelson.

"Why, sir, it lies but a few miles from here," said the Rev. Thomas Lancaster, vicar of Merton. "It is called the Surrey Iron Railway, and it crosses the road to London. There are trucks on lines drawn by horses, and they carry merchandise from Wandsworth to Croydon."

"Is there not a similar thing drawn by a steam engine?" asked the Rev. Nelson.

"There is indeed," was the reply. "Last year a man named Trevithick—he's the son of a Cornish mine manager—produced a thing he called a locomotive. I am told it hauled ten tons of iron and seventy workmen in a number of wagons at nearly five miles an hour over rails at a mine in South Wales."

"Do you think it could ever be used to take *passengers?*"

"Why, no. About four years ago Trevithick designed a steam carriage to run on the roads. This conveyed a load of

196

passengers. He called it The Puffing Devil. And devil it was, for it burned out while he and his friends were celebrating in an inn after its first run. No, sir, such things will never carry passengers."

Adkins turned from this conversation, for it did not seem that he would learn from it what he sought.

One of the gentlemen guests was talking animatedly a few yards away, and the detective moved closer.

"Deuced queer story my Lord Nelson was telling," this fellow was saying. "It appears that when my lord admiral was in the West Indies a long time ago he had his fortune told by a gypsy. She indicated everything that would happen to him up to this year."

"Up to this very year—1805?" asked a lady.

"That is so. The gypsy said she could see no *further* than this year."

Adkins thought the matter rather odd. But was it not just a silly old prophecy? And in any case the admiral was not in any personal danger now he was home from the sea . . .

The thief-taker rejoined the two parsons, who were now discussing some of the sea stories that the admiral had been recounting since his return.

"I hear that my lord was not fortunate enough to take part in the summer's only battle with a part of the French fleet," he said.

"That is quite true," said the admiral's brother. "My lord had chased the enemy to the West Indies and back, but as luck would have it he wasn't anywhere near in July when Sir Robert Calder's squadron of fifteen of the line came across Villeneuve one hundred miles west of Cape Finisterre."

The detective sipped wine and laid his glass on a small table. "It was a battle which took place, I understand, at long range and was somewhat indecisive. Do you think my lord admiral would have made better play of the situation, had he been fortunate enough to be in the vicinity?"

"Now, now, Mr. Adkins, do not make me boast about

my good brother. Who is to say? But bless my soul, maybe it is a good thing in one way that my lord had no part in it."

"Pray why, Mr. Nelson?"

"Your question is easily answered, Mr. Adkins. While my brother waited to come ashore at Portsmouth he sent me an express. In it he spoke of the battle, and this is what he wrote, for I remember his words precisely—*'If I had fallen in with them, you would probably have been a Lord before I wished; for I know they meant to make a dead set at the Victory'.*"

"England is indeed fortunate that they did not have that opportunity," remarked Adkins. "It would seem by the statement that they desired to kill him, and England cannot do without her Lord Nelson."

With the words Adkins dismissed this, too, from his mind, assuming that it was a somewhat natural thing for a famous commander-in-chief to write to his brother, specially when the admiral was of such a frank disposition.

There was to be a further example of Nelson's enthusiasm and openness—a dangerous one.

It occurred when a Captain Keats called to see him. The two sailors went to that part of the admiral's garden that had been made to resemble a quarter deck. And pacing there, Nelson confided to him the strategy he would employ when, please God, the great sea battle was joined.

These were his words: "When we meet them, as meet them we shall, I shall form the fleet into three divisions in three lines. One division shall be composed of twelve to fourteen of the fastest two-decked ships, which I shall keep always to windward, or in a situation of advantage; I shall put them under an officer who, I am sure, will employ them effectively, whether he has to take my orders or use his own.

"With the remaining part of the fleet formed in two lines, I shall go at them at once, if I can, about one-third of their line from their leading ship.

"I think it will surprise and confound the enemy. They won't know what I am about. It will bring forward a pell-mell battle, and that is what I want."

It was a plan typical of England's Nelson, of the man who had told Mr. Pitt, the prime minister, that the French and Spanish fleet must be "found and annihilated." It was also, as it so happened, a plan that had never been used before in the rules of naval warfare. Knowledge of it could, therefore, be of incalculable value to the enemy.

Despite this, the admiral revealed it also in a conversation with his old friend Addington.

And, of course, he told his dearest Emma.

That was how it came to the ears of Adkins—and of others more dangerous . . .

For Lady Hamilton took great pleasure in describing the plan in detail at table and in the drawing-room. "My dear Horatio is quite ready for the French . . . He has his strategy all made up, and it is quite, quite, brilliant . . . Dear Horatio, is he not very clever? He will form his fleet into three divisions . . ."

Adkins, listening to her, marvelled at such artlessness when England was at war. It was amazing, too, that her doting lover did not bid her hold her tongue.

The detective was not the only one to be excited by Lady Hamilton's indiscretion. For it did not take long for news of it to ring in the ears of the pecuniary Jedd Stickles, gossip of it having reached the kitchen by way of those who served at table.

The waiters, however, were somewhat dull of memory, and the details of the plan escaped them.

Stickles at once sought Jenny and led her to her room. "Get that plan, every word of it," he ordered. "It's worth a fortune in gold. Get it out o' milady."

"Fool, what would she tell *me* for?"

"Use your wits and she will. With your mem'ry, lass, you'll bring me every word."

Jenny used her wits.

199

It was not long before Nelson's battle plan was on its way to the men from France.

It may have been that Adkins sensed that something was afoot, for he asked permission of the admiral to send a servant with a letter to Bow Street. It was addressed to Mr. Day, and it read:

> *If any event of Importance is to occur in this Distinguished Household, then it cannot now be long delayed. I have heard it said that the Admiral may be wanted soon to go back to sea to take command of a Verie Important Event.*
>
> *The Admiralty, who are retaining my services, are being most generous in what they pay me. But how I wish I knew precisely what I was looking for.*
>
> *In these circumstances, I should deem it a great favour if you would come to this district and take up residence in a local inn.* The Fox and Grapes *is a good one.*
>
> *If you are near at hand, my friend, I think we should be well prepared for any event.*

Day took a room at the inn, and rode over to Merton Place to inform a gloomy Adkins of his arrival. "I have brought two of my patrol," he said, "and there are they who ride in this area should we require more. How go your inquiries, my dear fellow?"

"I have found nothing that might explain all the mysterious things that have happened," admitted the detective. "And what is so important to me—nothing that might lead me to Rosemary. I may as well admit it, Josiah, I am haunted day and night by the thought that something terrible has happened to her. Do you think she is still—alive?"

"Until you hear that she is not," said Day, gently, "try to put the best face on it."

"I shall try," was the answer. "But because of her, and what has happened to her, my work is no longer like a game, and it did once appear to be so."

"I understand," said Day. "Aye, more than most. Pray God you do not lose your lady—as I lost mine." He looked downwards for a moment and clenched his fists.

"If I did not know before what it meant to you, then I certainly do now," said Adkins. "A curse on the highway villain who did it. He should be shot with his own pistol."

"Just a little I had learned to live with it," said the conductor. "For a long time I had not spoken of it, but I have been led back of late to thinking on it—and Harry, I am convinced I have discovered something important. Important to me, anyhow."

"About the killing of your wife?"

"Aye. Maybe I should not speak of it at this moment. You are worried enough about—your own affairs."

"But, of course, Josiah. We are friends, are we not?"

"Aye, we are friends."

"Then speak out."

"I had meant to do so. The truth is, Harry, and it is quite remarkable, I think I know now who he is."

"He who—killed her?"

"Aye." Day paused, and it was as though he had to make an effort to continue. "Bickershaw!" he spat out.

"God in heaven! How have you discovered it?"

"I have been making inquiries on my own account. At the time I had been given a description of the villain, but in my sorrow I had not remembered it. However, something has been growing on me since that night when I took Bickershaw.

"At first I thought myself a fool, and did not say a word of it. But I was driven at last to pay calls on those who had shared the coach with her on that night. They told me again all they could remember about the scoundrel. And it fitted, Harry, it fitted well—even to the old sabre cut on his cheek."

"Josiah." Day gripped his friend's arm.

"I could not find the driver of the coach, but one who rode in it said he remembered the man swearing at the time that the rogue had the likeness of a character known to coachmen on the Portsmouth Road as—Gentleman Jerry."

"Josiah, this is most intriguing. It does much to prove our suspicions about Bickershaw's real trade, and we must catch him out at it."

"Pray God we do." Day's head was bowed, as though his words were indeed a prayer. Then he threw back his shoulders. "I shall be at the *Fox and Grapes*. A word and I shall be with you, day or night."

Gravely he rode back to the inn.

When he had gone Adkins fell to thinking about what his friend had told him. Then he remembered there was something he must do, for the sight of Lord Nelson preparing for a journey brought it back to mind.

The detective had known since the previous day that the admiral was to set off alone to visit his friend Addington, and had decided this would be the best time for him to do something that must be done—to put to Lady Hamilton some important matters of security.

It was one of the few bright, warm days in a summer that had been noted for much wind and rain, and the admiral took the open carriage, informing his driver to proceed slowly so that he might enjoy the country air.

It was an ideal day, too, for one John Bellamy, whose real name he had himself all but forgotten. Just twenty-four hours ago he and Justice had received a warning from that money-grubbing footman that Lord Nelson was to make the journey—and with it the most entertaining item of intelligence that had come their way for a long time.

" 'Tis astounding," had been the reaction of Justice, who was more used to dealing in intelligence than assassination. "The whole plan of action. In France, with this knowledge, I can make my name."

"Use it by all means," Bellamy had retorted. "But what we are about to do, and very soon, may to some extent cancel it out, unless those who may succeed him are in agreement with his plan."

Then they had gone to Bickershaw, and Bellamy had

said: "It is the road you say is best of all. Be ready to ride early, and show us the spot you would use."

So now the three horsemen lay in wait in a small wood that commanded the road for a great distance, lurking in its shadows like creatures that come to life by night.

"It is to be done today without fail," said Bellamy, and his face was darker than the shadows made it. "Remember well, Bickershaw, that you will earn by this day's work enough to live on for a lifetime."

Inexorably Admiral Lord Nelson's carriage trundled on. They would see it coming down the long, straight stretch, and they would be left in no doubt as to its occupant. For England's hero sat in solitary state, resplendent in his uniform, the sunlight glinting on his four medals of chivalry, marking the area of his heart.

CHAPTER TWENTY-FIVE

"I WOULD not presume on my position in this house as a guest," began Adkins, bowing to Lady Hamilton, "were it not of the utmost importance."

The admiral's lady, who was in her gayest mood, was prepared to make almost any concession. "You must speak as you please, my dear sir," she said. "But if it concerns the inquiries you have been making of late, would it not be preferable to await my lord's return and speak to *him* on the matter?"

"I fear it would not, my lady, for it is you to whom I wish to speak."

"Speak, then, by all means, sir."

The detective cleared his throat. "It is a somewhat delicate matter, and I should begin by saying that I am here as a guest for certain reasons of security. Because of this I have, I am afraid, been disturbed by certain statements you have made in this house in the hearing of quite a number of your guests."

"Oh? What statements, pray?"

"As I have said, it is a delicate matter. It is, in short, that you have set forth my lord admiral's plan of attack——"

"Do my ears play me false, sir? *My lord* has not objected. I do not see, therefore, why you——"

"I do not, my lady, speak without some authority. The Admiralty is concerned about some recent happenings, and least of which is the reason why your niece at this very moment is missing and is, no doubt, *in some considerable danger*. Sir Richard Ford, of Bow Street, is worried. And I, my lady, am quite beside myself for fear of Miss Hart. You are, of course, aware of the relationship that grew up between your niece and I."

Lady Hamilton put a hand gently on his arm. "I know,

Mr. Adkins. I know. Do not think that I am not vastly worried about her myself."

"Thank you, my lady." The thief-taker's eyes dropped, and he did not continue speaking for a time. "It is a trifle difficult for me, as you will appreciate. I am myself involved emotionally, yet I must keep my wits about me for what may be—even greater issues for England."

"I understand. But I cannot think that his lordship's battle plan can be anything but safe in this household and among his friends."

"Maybe not, my lady. But I would remind you that there are grave suspicions that French spies are at work attempting to gain information. We cannot trifle with such fellows, and have you not thought that the very walls of your drawing-room might have ears? I do think it would be wiser if you did not talk of the plan again—even to your friends."

"I promise, Mr. Adkins."

"Thank you. And now we have settled that, might I ask if you have told this plan to any others save those to whom I heard you speak?"

"One only."

"May I ask who?"

"My personal maid."

"Your personal maid!" Adkins was on his feet, aghast, almost stunned. "How did you come to tell *her?*"

"She heard from one of the servants who waits on table."

"In heaven's name, my lady, did I not tell you your walls may have ears?"

"But she showed such kindly interest. She has always done so."

The detective took a pace towards her. "Might I ask you what you mean by that last statement?"

"Merely that—that——" Her voice trailed away.

"I must insist on your answer."

"Merely that—she has always shown an interest in my lord's affairs at sea. She is a good girl. I—I read my lord's letters to her. She showed great appreciation."

"I do not doubt it. But I thought it was to Miss Hart you read those letters?"

"Only when my niece advised me to stop reading them to the maid. Only then I began to acquaint Rosemary of what my lord wrote."

Adkins was pacing the room, his hands clasped behind his back, his eyes narrowed in thought. His brain was searching for an answer that was near to dawning. This marching to and fro, this nervous movement helped him to think . . .

My lady's maid was deeply involved with that Stickles fellow. She had entered his bedroom in the most familiar manner, and no doubt they had other common interests apart from sex. For in all conscience Stickles had been more tied up with the murdered Jack Jumper than he had cared to say. And Jumper had known more than was good for him about the killing of Swift and Jamieson.

By God's name, there was at last a shaft of light. He would not have dreamt, in his wildest fancy, that the little lady's maid was the key to the mystery, and everything may now fall neatly into place. . .

He halted in his pacing, snapping his finger and thumb. He began to rap out orders, and there was no time now for titles and the niceties.

"Send for your maid. Do not on any account tell her that it is I who wants her. Send for two of your strongest gardeners. Cribb—I like the fellow—and one other. Have them attend me. Do not have a word said to your footman, Stickles. I shall bring him to this room myself, lest he decide to fly."

Without waiting for a reply, he went to his room, took a pair of handcuffs from his case and placed them in his pocket. Then he went to the kitchen, where he beckoned Stickles.

"Please to come with me," he said.

"Why?"

"You will learn soon enough."

When they entered the drawing-room, Jenny the maid was there with Lady Hamilton, who said to Adkins: "The two men you required have been sent for."

"Thank you. When they come send them in. And now, my lady, I should be obliged if you would leave us together."

When Lady Hamilton had left the detective placed his back to the door and launched into the most direct questions. The first he addressed to Jenny. "You gained information from the letters my lady read to you. To whom did you give that information?"

The effect upon Jenny was one of shock, and she remained tongue-tied.

"Answer girl, or it will go ill with you."

"I—I didn't give it to no one."

"You gave it to Stickles here. Come, my girl, you are most intimate with him, are you not?"

"Oh, sir!"

"Well? You are, are you not?"

The girl became hysterical. Believing that Stickles had betrayed her, she hurled herself upon him, beating at his chest with her fists. "You pig!" she screamed. "You've gone and told 'im."

Adkins stood still, allowing her to talk on.

She took a pace towards him. "First 'e told me it'd be all right, and now wot's 'appened? I've got a little bastard inside o' me, that's wot. Won't say he'll wed me neither."

"Shut yer mouth!" yelled Stickles.

"Shut yer own," retorted Jenny. "Said the other'd be all right, too. Said no 'arm could come o' givin' the gentleman word o' wot 'is lordship the admiral was about. Now 'e's got the law on me, and wot can a poor girl do?"

Adkins turned to Stickles. "Of your affairs in bed, neither I nor the law is interested. But the information you got from this girl, what use did you make of it?"

The footman was bewildered, silent.

"Come, sir, tell me what I wish to know—*and you may yet not hang.*"

"Sent it to two gentlemen." The footman's voice was almost inaudible.

"Their names, if you please?"

Again there was silence.

"Very well, Stickles, *I* will tell *you*. One is named Justice."

"Aye."

"And the other is a tall man, all of six feet, with a pale face. He has piercing eyes and seldom smiles, dark hair, big black eyebrows and big moustache. Am I not correct?"

"Aye."

"What does he call himself?"

"Bellamy. Mr. John Bellamy."

Adkins allowed himself a ghost of a smile. Now he had the man's name.

"I didn't see no 'arm." Shocked and frightened as he was, the footman's mock-refined speech had vanished, and he reverted to his more natural dialect. "Said 'e was a professor, 'e did. Wanted ter do some writin', so 'e said."

"So he said. In all my years I have not seen a man less like a professor. Stickles, you are an unconscionable fool. I wager all the writing *he* has done is to France. I suppose he paid well."

"Aye."

"And I suppose he is now in possession of my Lord Nelson's plan against the French?"

"Aye."

"Then you must have guessed in the end that the affair was less innocent than you suggest, but we will not for the time being waste time on that. What did they want to know in particular?"

"Anything wot we could find out about th' admiral. Like w'en 'e wus coming 'ome and that."

There was a knock on the door, and Adkins opened it to admit Cribb and his assistant.

Then the detective continued his interrogation. "Now, what about Jumper? I can guess now that he was working for those characters also?"

"Aye."

Adkins strode across to Stickles, and stared unblinkingly at him. "Where is Miss Hart? What have they done with her?"

"Dunno."

"Where is she?"

"I dunno. Honest I don't."

"All right, then, where do I find your friends Justice and Bellamy?"

"Never did know where they lived."

"If you *do* know, Stickles, you will tell me sooner than you think, for I shall make you. For the time being, hold out your wrists."

Stickles, from whom all spirit had drained, obeyed the order, and Adkins, taking the handcuffs from his pocket, manacled his prisoner.

Then the thief-taker addressed the two gardeners. "Take these two persons away—the stable, a garden shed, anywhere you think safe. Guard them well, for I shall have need of them further."

When he was alone Adkins continued his pacing. He felt somehow that there was still one thing missing. He allowed his mind to pass idly over recent events.

Suddenly his thoughts linked up. It was musing on the gypsy's prophecy that put him on the right trail. She had, in her way, seen his death in this very year . . . Nelson knew that if he met the French fleet they meant to "make a dead set at him," no doubt to despatch him, if possible, into the next world . . . Mr. John Bellamy, if that were his name, had wanted to know when the admiral was coming home . . .

Suddenly it was clear.

Assassination!

That was it. That was the desperate scheme.

He was hauling on the bell rope, not waiting for an answer, wrenching open the door and racing for the hall.

For was not Lord Nelson out on one of the loneliest roads, unguarded and with an unarmed driver, taking his first drive alone since his homecoming, and speeding peacefully through the summer's morning to his death.

It would be impossible to reach him in time, for he would be nearing the end of his journey. He had been gone a long time, and the detective feared that nothing could be done now to stay the hand that was raised to kill.

CHAPTER TWENTY-SIX

THOSE who had but a short acquaintance with the benign, ambling Adkins would never have believed he could move so rapidly—or issue orders so vociferously.

In the hall he was creating a hubbub, ringing more bells, shouting commands at servants who appeared from several directions at once.

"My Lady Hamilton. Bring her here. The fastest curricle. Get it ready. I want he to drive who is not afraid of danger. A brace of pistols and well primed. Fetch me a groom to ride with a message . . .

"Ah, my lady. His lordship's precise destination. The road he has taken. Quickly."

His hostess supplied the information as the groom arrived.

"You heard her ladyship?" Adkins asked the man. "Post to the *Fox and Grapes* without delay. My compliments to Mr. Day. Tell him I have gone on along that road, and ask him to follow pell-mell."

He was through the door and on the steps, turning for an instant to shout to Lady Hamilton: "No time to explain. 'Tis too urgent."

Then he was racing for the stables, where two horses were being put in the shafts of a low, racy curricle, a footman running after him with the pistols.

He was off down the drive and wheeling into the road-way. "Use your whip. Get 'em stepping as smart as can be."

The pace increased. The curricle jolted and swayed, all but turning over. But still over the pounding and rattling Adkins demanded more and more speed, and for the man who handled the reins it was his wildest drive.

Adkins, sitting grimly, watched the hedgerows flying and the road racing up to meet them and spinning out behind.

On the open plain the wind whipped about his ears. Under a roof of tree branches it was in reality too dim for their hurtling speed.

It was impossible to reach the admiral in time. But it was worth the try.

The curricle whirled on . . .

Ahead Nelson's carriage moved slowly up a long, winding hill. The admiral was in no haste, and his driver slackened rein and allowed the horses to plod.

The long watch at sea had not helped his constitution, but the days at Merton had animated him. His country house held all that was dear to him in his personal life; but there was room in his heart to love England more.

Scarcely home, he had attended no less than fourteen conferences in London, and he was ready to weigh anchor again as soon as his services might be required.

It was one of those perfect days that England, even in an uncertain summer, can produce like a miracle. The birds flew and sang. A dazzling sun had warmed away the mist. And he was on his way to see an old friend.

His carriage rolled on.

But over the rise he would come into the view of those who waited for him, and remain so on the long sweep down towards them.

Bellamy's horse was restless, and he more so. Would the man never come? They had certain knowledge that he would be on this road and alone.

They knew him to be an early riser, and their information was that he would begin his journey soon after he had breakfasted. If the appearance of his carriage were delayed much longer there might be more traffic, even for this lonely stretch, than they wished for.

Now that the time had come Bellamy wished to get to grips with that which had to be done. He was not the man to be nervous, but it was too near to the moment for which he had worked.

They wore black masks, and no smile beneath them, for they were men who waited to perpetrate an act of violence in cold blood.

Time lay heavy.

Bellamy broke a long silence. "You know what to do?" he asked.

"Yes," said Justice in a strained voice, "we know what to do."

"Well see to it that nothing goes wrong."

"Nothing will go wrong."

"It is to appear like a hold-up," explained Bellamy, for the fifth time in an hour. "We are to seem like highway robbers."

"Won't be difficult for me," said Bickershaw, "for I *am* one, don't you know?"

"You will do the talking, Bickershaw, for you have the lingo. Do not worry if your voice be known, for we shall take you to a good life in France. We do not wish to fire while moving, for our aim will be more accurate while standing still.

"We shall all fire at once and at my command. The three of us, with two pistols each, cannot fail to accomplish the task with absolute accuracy.

"The driver we shall allow to escape, so that he will tell a tale of three highway robbers, and it will go down in history as nothing more."

There was another long silence.

"A carriage!" Bellamy picked it out first as it topped the rise.

"Is it him?" breathed Justice.

Bellamy shaded his eyes as the vehicle began its descent. He did not speak until he was certain. "It is him," he said.

They could see the famous admiral, pale faced and half-smiling in the sunshine. He seemed so delicate a figure that his despatch would surely be the easiest task in the world.

"Why does he not hurry?" said Justice, gaunt and grey behind his black mask.

213

The carriage advanced slowly. But it came nearer and nearer . . .

"Now!" exclaimed Bickershaw.

The three horsemen moved abreast out of the wood and halted at one side of the road.

"Stand—or you're a dead man!" roared Bickershaw at the driver, who raised his whip for a moment, changed his mind because the carriage could not have picked up speed quickly, and hauled on the reins instead. The vehicle drew in to the other side of the road.

"What is the meaning of this?" shouted the admiral, remaining seated and relaxed as though he interviewed a junior officer in his own cabin.

"It be Gentleman Jerry, or I'm a blind 'un," said the coachman over his shoulder. "A noted highway robber, my lord. I could tell the cut o' his jib anywhere."

"That will be quite enough tongue from you, my lad," bellowed Bickershaw. "I'll relieve you o' your money—or you're both dead mutton this instant——"

They became conscious suddenly of a pounding and rattling, of a man's voice yelling above the noise to attract their attention away from what they were at. Bearing down on them was a curricle with a tall driver and a smaller passenger.

For a moment Adkins's driver tightened his hold on the reins because the three horsemen, on one side of the road, were in his way and he might collide with them.

The thief-taker stopped shouting at the horsemen in front and bawled in his driver's ear. "Faster! Faster! Use your whip. Run 'em down."

"We'll go over if we hit 'em, sir."

"To hell with turning over," yelled Adkins. "Drive straight at 'em."

They did drive straight at them, careering faster, the horses almost out of control, Adkins yelling like a demon to distract them further.

Two of them *were* diverted, for this was surely a madman.

Justice and Bickershaw took their eyes from the admiral and directed them at the flying curricle. Then, recognizing the little Runner, they turned their pistols upon him instead of their quarry.

Not so the third horseman. For Bellamy even death would be preferable to failure. And he was taking aim at the admiral.

The shots of the two who aimed at Adkins thudded into the woodwork of the curricle. That of Bellamy embedded itself in a tree at the other side of the road. For his horse moved suddenly in the din, and Nelson was leaping from his carriage in the confusion.

At the last moment the three horsemen wheeled away from the galloping danger hurtling down on them.

At that moment, too, the terrified animals that bore down on them swerved, reared and plunged . . . And over went the curricle. But before it did Adkins found his eyes staring at the scarf of one of the horsemen, not two yards away, and he thrust forward both his pistols and exploded them.

The curricle was on its side, its two occupants in a bed of nettles and wild flowers under the hedge.

Bellamy and Justice were still mounted, their pistols either discharged or torn from their grasp, but their swords were in their hands ready to do with them as much mischief as they could.

But there was a new thunder, rolling from the direction the curricle had come. A little group of figures in blue had topped the rise, one slightly ahead of the others, in a formation Bellamy knew of old. They were riding like the cavalry men they were, no man moving an inch from his station, and it was as wild a charge on a rustic English highway as on the bloodiest field of Europe.

"Draw sabres!" Above the clatter Day's command was scarcely heard. But it was understood, and white gauntleted hands shot upwards to point glittering steel at the sky.

Day had only three of his men, including one who patrolled in the Wimbledon area, but the noise and dust they raised made them seem like a platoon. The men from France, their plans already upset, did not delay. From this new sight they spurred away to the south.

Day's little group halted. The admiral and his driver were safe, as were also Adkins and his driver, if somewhat winded and prickled.

One man lay dead, shot twice in the chest by Adkins. Jerry Bickershaw had stopped his last traveller. Not for him were to be a rich prize and a flight to France.

Thief-taker and conductor stood side by side looking down at the crumpled figure. Both of Adkins's shots had been lucky, for there were two wounds in the highwayman's chest.

On the detective's face was a strange, almost unbelieving look. Day's was working with emotion.

"Who did it?" he said at last, his voice almost a whisper.

"I did," said Adkins.

"Thank you," said Day, and his voice was rising, his shoulders squaring. "One of those shots was for me."

Then Day was taking command of the situation, despatching two of his men in pursuit of the Frenchmen, and ordering the others to manhandle the curricle back on to its wheels.

Little damage was done, and the driver was able to set off in it back to Merton, while Adkins mounted Bickershaw's horse and with Day and his two men escorted the admiral on his way.

After a time the two patrolmen who had ridden on cantered back. They had failed to find the Frenchmen.

"All in all, a good day's work," said Day, "though not quite perfect, for those two devils have got away."

The Little Ferret did not reply. He gazed down the empty road with an odd fixity, like a blind man. Aye, the two devils had got clean away, taking with them his last chance of finding Rosemary or what they might have done with her.

CHAPTER TWENTY-SEVEN

WHEN the patrol had seen Lord Nelson safely to his destination they left two men to escort him home and turned back towards Merton.

Adkins rode in silence. Gone were the smile from his face and the sparkle from his eyes. But suddenly he was stiffening in the saddle and putting heels to his horse.

"Come!" he called to the others. "That fool Stickles might have some meagre clue as to where they may hide. If he has we'll *make* him remember."

Riding hard dulled his fear that he may never see Rosemary again—and the pain.

"You have done well," shouted Day.

"I have not done well enough," returned Adkins above the din of their hooves. "I still have someone to find, if she be still——" The meaning was all too plain, and he did not finish his words.

At last they were drawing rein before the steps of Merton Place, dismounting and shouting for the prisoners to be brought to the hall.

"Stay with me, if you will, Josiah," said the detective. "Your uniform may frighten him the more."

Stickles was brought to the hallway, where Adkins paced.

"Is there any place they may hide?" demanded the thief-taker. "You must put your mind to it."

"Never knew where they lodged," replied the sullen footman. "Told you before, I have."

"I do not ask where they *lodged*. I wish to know where they may *hide*."

"How could I know? I was but a tool——"

"You were a *fool*. Please to *think*, man. Stir your brains."

Stickles shook his head. "Honest, sir, I just can't."

217

"Please to try. Tell me where they may be, and it may go better with you. Remember that, Stickles."

The footman hung his head.

"What can I do to stir your brain? What about Jumper? Did *he* know their haunts—not that he, poor fellow, can help us now."

"Jumper knew no more'n me."

"What about he they called Gentleman Jerry? He was in this up to his neck. Did *he* know? Did *he* tell you where they may be found?"

"Ah, Jerry——" The prisoner began to speak and then closed his mouth again, but there was a gleam in his eyes.

"Come, Stickles. You can speak of Bickershaw, for he's as dead as mutton."

"I'd forgot, but it's coming back to me."

"What's coming back, eh?" Adkins was almost whispering the words, fearful that what the man's mind clutched for might vanish.

"Well, Jerry was off to see 'em. Said he was going to— now where was it?"

"Try to remember. Try hard."

"Got it. Said he was riding south to a place near the sea. *Not far from Dungeness and near to the Romney Marshes.*"

"Did he give—a name, a house, an inn?"

"He did not."

"Never mind. At last we know where to look. Stickles, I thank you. Josiah, we have no time to lose."

They waited only for the thief-taker's two discharged pistols to be exchanged for fresh ones. Then they were on the road again, the four grim-faced policemen, riding hard and in silence as though nothing could stop them until they reached the sea.

It was late when the two Frenchmen dismounted at the shadowy porch of *The Seabird.*

When their horses flagged they had been forced to change them at an inn, and they had been given fresh but slower mounts. Now their flight to France was further held up, for the landlord swore that he would have to wait for the tide.

"A pox on our efforts," said Bellamy. "We did not get my lord admiral."

"No," said Justice, "but we got his battle plan, and I for one think it is an excellent second best."

"Well, get you on to the ship at once with the words well remembered in your head. As you say, we have at least got that, so get it safely aboard in your person for fear we are pursued." Bellamy sat down heavily. "I shall remain here for a while. There are some papers to be burned, and I want some time to think. I may yet stay behind when you sail——"

"Do not be a fool. He will be well guarded by now."

"I may yet try again. In any event, as things are I do not know if I care to return to France. But get you gone in case they ride this way. The ship's captain must go aboard with you and be ready to sail at a moment."

"What about the girl?"

"You must not be delayed getting on the ship. Speed and I shall bring her. Or, if I do not come, then Speed will do so."

Justice moved towards the door, and Bellamy halted him for a moment. "One thing more, Charles. If you should hear the noise of pursuit, or pistols popping, or any such before we have joined you, you are not to wait for us, but you are to weigh anchor at once. That is an order."

"Do not delay long," said Justice, joining the skipper in the shadowy porch and disappearing with him into the darkness beyond.

Bellamy sat for a long time at the bare table, his head propped in his hands. Then, abruptly, he made up his mind. "Come, Speed," he said. "Get the girl."

Speed tied Rosemary's hands and then looped the end of a rope around her waist so that he would not lose her in the darkness. Bellamy carried a lantern.

An old servant of the smuggler's skipper opened the door

219

for them. He was a man with a grained, mahogany face who spoke only when he was addressed and gave the impression of being quite dumb.

"If any should come," said Bellamy, "you have never seen us. Do not tell them—anything."

Before they bent their heads towards the wind and the hill path, they paused to listen. Back down the long road over the moor there was no sound or echo of hooves, only the yaup of a sea-bird and the noise of the servant bolting the door behind them. There was little hope now that any would come in time. But for Rosemary Hart hope had already died in the burning, tearing torture to which Jeremiah Bickershaw had subjected her.

The four policemen changed their horses at an inn, where Adkins plied both landlord and ostlers with questions.

Yes, they had called earlier, the same two gentlemen, changing their horses and impatient to be off. Aye, away to the south east they'd gone.

How long since? God in heaven, that long ago . . .?

As impatient as they who had gone before, the four policemen were off again pounding the road.

"I fear we are too late." The words came again and again into the detective's head, echoing to the rhythm of the drumming hooves. But the words did not escape from his lips, which were tightly and grimly closed.

In the dark night *The Seabird* was a dead inn lost on a lifeless moor. The windows were shuttered, doors barred.

"As likely a place as ever I saw," said Adkins, "and not far from Dungeness, I'll wager." They were the first words he had spoken in those weary miles.

They fell to belabouring the door, first with fists, then with truncheons and sabres, and at last it was opened by the mahogany-faced servant. They strode in, brushing him aside. They marched from room to room.

In one there were a case lying open, spilling shirts and cravats, four discarded pistols, all requiring priming, ashes in the grate where papers had been burned—and a small piece of pink material torn from a lady's dress.

Adkins pounced on it, held it before the servant's eyes, thrust a pistol into the man's chest. "Where have they taken her?" he roared. "Speak—or I'll send you to perdition."

The man did not speak. But slowly he raised an arm and extended a finger. He did not need to speak, for to Adkins the meaning was very plain. To him, suddenly, the man was not pointing at the window but through it, through the dusty panes and away to the cliffs, and beyond that to the sea . . .

They did not wait even for a lantern, but raced from the inn and along the cliff path. Down in the bay was a dark smudge. Was it moving out to sea?

They began the descent to the beach down the twisting, tortuous path, and the distant surge of the sea sounded very cold in the windy dark.

The night was brightening. The clouds, which had seemed becalmed, began to sail. And the moon shone. The smudge in the bay was a small vessel. A boat was rowing out from it to the beach, and three figures waited on the sand. Two were dark cloaked, the third in a pale, flimsy garment blown by the wind.

For the figures on the sands the moon glinted also up on the rock-bound path, on polished leather and bits of steel moving down towards them.

John Bellamy at once discharged a pistol upwards into the air.

Slowly the boat, half-way to the beach, turned and began to row back to the ship.

The four policemen came on down, scrambling faster. Bellamy and Speed kicked off their boots, raced into the water and began to strike out. If they were lucky they might reach the rowing boat before it got to the ship.

Between them and the policemen stood Rosemary, stumbling on the sand, and they could not fire in case they hit her.

At last she fell into Adkins's arms as the three patrolmen ran on to the water's edge.

Day carried a carbine, and he raised it and took careful aim. When he fired John Bellamy, *Capitaine le Vicomte de St. Remy*, sank dead into the water. The other two patrolmen were shooting, too, but one of the figures, that of Speed, was to swim on and reach the small boat.

They were to know that it was Bellamy they had killed, for his body was to be washed up on the beach.

The little smuggler was soon moving out to sea, slowly but surely creaking and rolling into the night, and the little group of people on the beach had to stand and watch her go.

Justice stood in the stern gazing at the fading shore, and his brow was clear. It was difficult for a moment to realize that the man who had come to kill was himself dead. But above all other considerations he who had been Charles Justice, and could now be M. André Carillon again, member of Napoleon's special spy service, was now absolved of any further assistance in a mission he had never really wished to help.

Instead, he was returning to France with the most important single piece of intelligence that had ever come his way.

Softly and tensely, he began to repeat the exciting words. *"I shall form the fleet into three divisions in three lines . . ."*

At this moment the sea wind, cooling his face, was whipping away his voice as though his lips moved and yet he did not speak. But it would not be long before Admiral Villeneuve had those very words in his possession.

Not that it was to do Villeneuve, or France, a great deal of good . . .

Less than a fortnight was to pass before September 14th, when Nelson, still very much alive, was to arrive in Portsmouth to embark for the great battle. In the crowd that was to watch him go folk were to kneel down before him, and many were to be in tears. He sailed thinking of his mistress Emma and his daughter Horatia.

Soon, too, Lady Hamilton was to read out a letter from him that would have been of no value whatsoever to an enemy spy:

My dearest beloved Emma, the dear friend of my bosom,
The Signal has been made that the Enemy's Combined fleet are coming out of Port. We have very little wind, so that I have no hopes of seeing them before tomorrow. May the God of Battles crown my endeavours with success, at all events I will take care that my name shall ever be most dear to you and Horatia, both of whom I love as much as my own life, and as my last writing before the Battle will be to you, so I hope God that I shall live to finish my letter after the Battle. May Heaven bless you, prays your

Nelson and Brontë

Nelson was not to be the man to alter his plan, for he wanted nothing if not "a pell-mell battle". This he got, even though the enemy knew beforehand what he was about. And more, much more . . .

He was not himself to live through the battle. But Trafalgar was to be his. His and England's. And the greatest naval victory in history.

Before Nelson went to his glory and his doom, however, two less famous British subjects had a very important matter to discuss.

It was the night the smuggler sailed with the French spy. When she had slipped away they who had reached the beach just in time to save Rosemary made their way with her in darkness and silence back up the winding path.

In *The Seabird* a warm fire and hot drinks helped Rosemary's shocked condition, but brought her back to life and sadness.

"I cannot ever be yours," she cried out at last. Her voice was impassioned, her eyes wild.

"You have no choice," he said, "for I shall never let you go."

"Oh you will, Harry, you will. You will not see me again when I tell you that I was his, that Bickershaw's—by force."

It was good for her that she was crying, and he allowed her to do so for a long time.

"I think I should tell you," he said then, "that I have killed Bickershaw with my own hand. Do you not think, my dear, that this has evened up the score?"